ALIBI FOR A WI

Nothing was out of place. Nothing looked strange or unusual.

It was such a relief to Ruth that at last tears overcame her completely. She dropped into a chair, buried her face in her arms and gave herself up to sobs.

The sensation of it was wonderful. Shock and terror seemed to drain out of her with the streaming tears. She was crying so unrestrainedly that she did not hear a footstep in the hall.

But she heard when the voice of Marguerite Ranzi remarked thoughtfully from the doorway, 'So you care all that much, do you? Lester only laughed about it, of course, but I often wondered. . . .'

Alibi For A Witch

Elizabeth Ferrars

CORONET BOOKS
Hodder and Stoughton

> 'Where hast thou been, sister?'
> 'Killing swine.'
> 'Sister, where thou?'
>
> **Macbeth**

Copyright © 1952 by M. D. Brown

First published in Great Britain in 1952 by William Collins Sons & Co. Ltd.

Reissued in 1991 by Constable and Company Ltd.

Coronet edition 1993

British Library C.I.P.

A CIP catalogue record for this book is available from the British Library

ISBN 0 340 57408 9

Printed and bound in Great Britain for Hodder and Stoughton Paperbacks, a division of Hodder and Stoughton Ltd, Mill Road, Dunton Green, Sevenoaks, Kent TN13 2YA (Editorial Office: 47 Bedford Square, London WC1B 3DP) by Clays Ltd, St Ives plc.

I

THAT DAY began in the same way as so many others, though perhaps the quarrel at breakfast between Lester Ballard and the boy Nicky was a little worse than usual, and perhaps Ruth Seabright was drawn into it further than she usually allowed herself to be drawn into those violent and unpleasant scenes; at any rate, Madge Gargiulo, clearing the table on the terrace and showing some grim amusement at it all, gave Ruth a good-humoured warning to be careful how she mixed herself up in the life of her employer. But all this was so similar to what happened two or three times a week in the white villa on the cliffs that there was really no reason for Ruth to feel as upset as she did. For four years she had schooled herself to think as little as possible about the antagonism between Lester Ballard and his son and with time had become so accustomed to it that usually she almost thought of it as normal. All the same, on that day when Nicky had gone off, white-faced, to his room, and Lester Ballard, laughing and with an excited gleam in his eyes, had walked out to his car and driven away towards San Antioco with the two Gargiulos, Ruth found that her heart, all of a sudden, was beating distinctly faster than it should.

She did not know why she should be frightened. The things that had been said and the things that had been done had been the same as the things said and done in that house times without number. Yet, as she found herself alone at the table on the terrace, gazing towards the mountains afloat in mist on the far side of the glittering bay, Ruth felt that only the worst blindness and stupidity had saved her until then from seeing the dangers in the situation.

Soon, of course, she recovered. But for a while she had been so lost in her own emotions that afterwards she was quite unable to say for sure when certain things had happened.

For instance, she had not noticed when Nicky left the house. She did not know either when the man in the checked shirt and blue cotton trousers had first sat down on the low wall beside the road and began his long scrutiny of the villa.

She noticed the man only when she got up from the table to answer the telephone. She saw him then, sitting on the wall, cupping his hands round a match to light a cigarette. But his head was bent over the flame so that she could not see his face properly and at that moment he made hardly any impact on her thoughts. In fact, by the time that she had reached the telephone, she had forgotten having seen him. It was Mrs. Ranzi on the telephone.

She said, " I rang up to remind you about this afternoon, Ruth." Her voice had a singing quality that made it sound almost Italian, though she had been born and bred in Sussex. " You're coming, aren't you ? "

For a moment Ruth could not remember what was to happen that afternoon. Then she said, " This afternoon— oh, yes."

" You hadn't forgotten, had you ? "

" No, of course not."

There was a pause, then Marguerite Ranzi asked, " Is something the matter ? You sound queer, somehow."

" No," Ruth said, " only there's been another of those horrible scenes between Lester and Nicky. . . . Marguerite, I'm going to leave. I don't think I can stand it here any longer."

" Leave ? Go back to England ? "

" Or to another job."

" But you can't do that. You mustn't. Just think of me. I've got to have someone of my own sort to talk to now and again."

It amused Ruth to hear Marguerite Ranzi describe her as her own sort. Their friendship, if it could be called that, had been born of little but their proximity in a place where few other English people stayed for long.

" Someone else will turn up," Ruth assured her. " Apart from anything, I've got practically nothing to do now. I'm frightfully bored."

" Well, but think of Nicky," Marguerite said. " Not that I can bear the creature, but you've been gradually turning him into something almost human, whereas Lester, poor dear, hasn't the faintest idea what to do about him."

" At the moment," Ruth said, " I could cheerfully murder poor, dear Lester."

" Well, so could I at times," Marguerite said. " He's a vain little man and vain people shouldn't have children. Only he's so attractive in his rather impossible way."

" I've never been able to see it."

This was not strictly true. For the first few months of her employment as governess, or adopted aunt, or general good influence for the boy Nicky, Ruth had been strongly attracted by the elder Ballard. But his treatment of his son had cured her remarkably quickly, far more quickly than she would have been cured by his indifference to herself. Most of her own childhood had been fatherless, which had left her with an idealistically clear-cut conception of what the love of a father ought to be.

" He's got a shabby, sadistic passion for rousing Nicky's rages," she said. " It's always Lester who starts it. Just when everything's peaceful and pleasant, he turns to me with a gay and amusing little story of something silly that Nicky's said or done. Then he waits. I know that look in his eyes while he's waiting. And Nicky tries not to rise to it, but sits there getting whiter and whiter and trying not to say anything. Incidentally, that's new in him, the idea that it's worth trying to control himself. But I rather think the outburst, when it comes, is worse than it used to be. That's to say, it isn't exactly an outburst any more. It's much quieter, but it's as if it meant more." She stopped, beginning to feel annoyed with herself for having talked about the morning's quarrel. She was not in the habit of confiding in Marguerite. " Well, I dare say I'm exaggerating it all," she said, " because I lost my own temper and told Lester a little of what I think of him."

Marguerite laughed, a deep, throaty laugh. " That won't do him any harm. And he won't mind, either. I expect it amused him."

" Of course it amused him ! " Ruth dropped her attempt not to talk. " He laughed like anything and went off this morning with his eyes shining with beastly pleasure."

" He's gone in to Naples, has he ? "

" Yes, thank heaven. With the two Gargiulos. It's their day off, so I've got the place to myself to calm down in. I hate losing my temper."

Again Marguerite laughed. "This row this morning, was it about anything in particular?"

"Not really. I don't think so."

"Yet there was something special about it, to get you so upset."

Ruth did not answer at once. Then she said, "It felt different. More as if—no, that's silly."

"What were you going to say?"

"I was going to say, more as if something were going to happen because of it."

"What could happen?"

"Nothing, I suppose. I know I'm being silly. But I honestly think I've had as much of it as I can stand. I'm going to leave."

"You won't, of course," Marguerite said. "You know that would be the end of Nicky, and poisonous brat that he is, that would be a pity. Or you'd think it a pity. Myself, I could be quite indifferent on that point. Well, about this afternoon. You're coming along to have tea, aren't you?"

"Oh, yes."

"Come early, then. Come about three o'clock."

Ruth agreed, and Marguerite repeating, "Three o'clock," rang off.

It was only as Ruth put down the telephone that it occurred to her to wonder if Nicky might not still be in the house. He ought to have left it half an hour before to go to the house of Signor Bruno, the ex-university professor who was half-heartedly giving Nicky a little education, but Ruth had no memory of having heard him leave. Wondering with misgivings whether or not he had overheard what she had said to Marguerite on the telephone, Ruth looked up the well of the staircase and called out, "Nicky!"

There was no reply. She called twice more, then decided that after all the boy had gone.

She went out to the terrace again.

The day when the two Gargiulos, cook-housekeeper and chauffeur-gardener at the villa, had their day off together and Ruth had the place to herself, was usually the day of the week that she liked best. Crossing to the table where she had left her cigarettes, she sat down, lit a cigarette and let her gaze settle once more on the bay and the mountains beyond it. From the way that the mist enfolded them, revealing only their peaks, which seemed to be made of some ethereal stuff, shot through with light and floating in mid-air, she knew that the day was going to become intensely hot. But for the present it was reasonably cool on the terrace in the shade of a trellis covered with wistaria and passiflora.

The wistaria had almost finished its blossoming. Only a few mauve clusters dangled from the thickly growing greenery. It was so entwined with the passiflora, with its small, round, golden fruits, that they seemed to belong to the same plant. A big lizard clung motionless to one of the wooden laths of the trellis.

That man out there, Ruth thought, as she sat and smoked and realised that her talk with Marguerite had calmed her down, looked as if already he was finding the day unpleasantly hot. He looked uncomfortable. He looked restless and impatient. He did not look like a man who has sat down on a sun-warmed wall to smoke a cigarette for the sheer pleasure of doing that and for no other reason.

It was as this thought struck Ruth that she remembered that he had been there already when she had got up to go to the telephone.

He was a smallish, slight man with skin darkly tanned but with fair hair and thick, fair eyebrows that had been bleached almost white by the sun. His face was thin and he had small, unremarkable features. He was wearing a checked shirt with the sleeves rolled up above the elbows, faded blue cotton trousers and a pair of stained and battered canvas shoes. Through one of the buttonholes of his shirt he had stuck a sprig of bougainvillea.

As if he felt Ruth's attention upon him, he looked up with a sharp, questioning glance and, for a moment, she had the feeling that he meant to speak to her. But turning his head away, he looked down the road towards San Antioco. Ruth got up and went indoors again.

She went upstairs to her bedroom. The window was shuttered and the light inside was dim, so that the room had a look of coolness, even though the air was heavy with the heat. Her reflection in the looking-glass had a shadowy pallor. But when she pushed at one of the shutters to let in more light, the reflection brightened. Stripping off her clothes, she put on her swimming costume. Deep sunburn extended all over her slim back and shoulders and up her slender thighs. She was naturally rather dark skinned and she had tanned smoothly and attractively. Her straight, thick hair was dark also and so were her eyes, with long, thick, black lashes. Yet in spite of this Southern colouring, Ruth was always instantly recognised as English. She had grown up in London and had never been able to conceal the fact. Sometimes this annoyed her. In a land of beautiful women, she would have liked to be able occasionally to pass herself off as a Latin. But it never happened.

Putting on a blue cotton dress over her swimming costume, tying a red and white handkerchief over her hair and putting on a pair of sun-glasses, she collected a writing pad, her fountain pen and a towel and went downstairs again. She remembered to close and lock the doors of the villa before she left it. Usually, when she was merely going for a swim, she would not have troubled to do this, but something about the man, sitting out there on the wall, waiting restlessly for something or other to happen, prompted her for once to make sure that all the doors and the shutters of the ground-floor windows were fastened.

The man was still there when she went down the steps between the big agaves and the bright bushes of oleander to the road. On hearing her, he looked round quickly and again his sharp, questioning glance dwelt on her face. Under his thick, pale eyebrows his eyes were a greenish grey. They struck Ruth as furtive and anxious.

For a moment she again had the impression that he was about to speak to her, but either she was mistaken or else something about her made him change his mind. Throwing away the match that he had just used to light another cigarette, he thrust both hands into his pockets, jingling some coins there. Ruth passed him, going towards San Antioco, swinging her towel. Just before the bend in the road hid the man from her, she glanced back and noticed that he appeared to have dropped his freshly-lighted cigarette in the road and to be grinding it out under his heel.

II

THE PATH to the sea turned off the road only a few yards
farther on, almost opposite the brightly-painted green doors
of the Ballards' garage. At the corner between the road
and the path was the village shop. A fat old woman was
sitting in its doorway beside piles of water-melons and
baskets of tomatoes, oranges and aubergines. She gave
Ruth a smile that showed dazzling teeth and called out
a greeting.

The path led steeply downwards past some cottages and
through some olive groves. It was paved with big, uneven
stones. At a turn in the path, Ruth passed a herd of goats
with broad wooden collars, pressing themselves against the
wall for shade. A bare-footed child with a dark, lovely face
was in charge of the goats. Smiling up at Ruth tentatively
as she went by, he murmured a soft-voiced, "Hallo."

Seen though the grey-green leaves of the olive trees, the
sea looked even more intensely blue than when it could be
seen unbroken, meeting the sky. Where the olive groves
ended, the paving ended too and a rough path, dropping
still more steeply, led down to a flight of worn, stone steps,
which were slippery with dust. Below was a narrow cove
with a sheer cliff on one side of it and sloping rocks on
the other. The water was clear and still, always a strangely
vivid green at its edge.

Not many people came there as a rule, but to-day some
young boys were talking and laughing noisily on one of the
higher ledges of rock. They dived into the water and
climbed out again with a great deal of splashing and shouting.
Ruth went to a low rock just above the water's edge and,
slipping out of her blue dress, sat down and dabbled her
feet in the warm ripples.

That group of boys, she thought, was extraordinarily
beautiful, even if they reminded her, by their chattering
and supple scampering on the rocks, of baboons on the
Mappin Terraces.

At that age, Nicky also had had the same grace and charm

and would have looked just as enchanting as any of those boys, diving and playing. With boys like that too, peasant boys from the cottages above, he would not have been self-conscious, but would have been happy and madly gay and popular. It was only among the educated, the people whom he expected to sneer at him for being slow and stupid, that he became moody and inept, overwhelmed by his own belief in his failure with them. Perhaps, since his Italian mother had died, Ruth had been the only person of his own class with whom Nicky had not had this feeling of failure, who had taken pains to make sure that he should not have it. Her reward had been Nicky's passion of love and gratitude, of which, however, she was only half-aware, being one of those people who find it hard to think of themselves as very lovable. She thought of Nicky as being too dependent on her, far too dependent for a boy of sixteen, and when a suspicion slid into her mind that there was something in the quality of Nicky's love which might make him ready to die for her or commit crimes for her, she treated this thought contemptuously as being merely the product of her own desire to be loved in that way, even if it was only by poor Nicky. Yet it was a fact that this suspicion had entered her mind before that morning. Before the quarrel that had left behind her mood of fear, Ruth had often thought of Nicky as capable of committing a crime. Not a crime of greed or of cunning, neither of which had any place in his nature, but a crime of violence. Later, this fact was of great importance.

She spent the morning alternately swimming and lying in the sun, putting off beginning the letter that she was intending to write. But at last she began it. The letter was to a girl who had been a friend of hers in the A.T.S. during the war, and who was now a partner in a small travel agency in London. It had occurred to Ruth to tell this friend that she was considering returning to England and to ask if a job might not be found for her in the agency.

This idea seemed to Ruth a good one, yet as she began a sentence in which she got as far as the word " returning " her pen hesitated. While minutes passed, the rest of the sheet of paper stayed blank.

Behind her a voice said, " I'm like that, too, about letters. I hate writing anything I don't expect to get paid for."

Ruth started and looked round.

It was Stephen Evers, who had come up quietly and now sat down beside her.

Ruth put down the pad and pen. As usual, her first thoughts on seeing Stephen were that he ought to have his hair cut and that a man as blond and bony as he was always looked a little absurd in swimming trunks in the hot sun. Even after two months at San Antioco he had achieved only an uneven reddening of the skin and a crop of freckles.

She did not like Stephen much. Yet she had nothing particular against him, except that she was fairly sure that he had no interest in her but only sought her out from time to time because she was an acquaintance of Marguerite Ranzi's.

Leaning back and supporting himself on his sharp elbows, he asked, " Was it a very difficult letter to write ? It looked as if it had brought on a profound depression."

" It wasn't the letter that did that," Ruth said. " I was thinking of something else and couldn't keep my mind on what I was supposed to be writing."

" Like me, most of the time. Only you don't depend on it. D'you know, I wish I could get a job like yours. I think it'd suit me. I'd be quite ready to mother half a dozen mentally deficient kids if it meant I could lead a carefree existence like yours in a place like this. Incidentally, do you ever have to do any actual work ? "

Ruth looked at him thoughtfully before she answered and stopped herself saying several of the things that came to her mind. Then she asked, " Who told you Nicky Ballard was mentally deficient ? "

" Isn't he ? " Stephen asked.

" Who told you he was ? "

" Oh, I don't know. Ballard, probably. And people in general. I've hardly spoken to him myself, though when I tried, it didn't go too well. I couldn't get a word out of him and he scowled at me as if I'd done him an injury."

" He's violently and miserably shy," Ruth said.

" Poor kid. Can't anything be done about it ? " Stephen asked negligently.

" For instance ? "

Something in her tone caught his attention but he misinterpreted it. " Look, I believe I broke in on you at a critical point in that letter, didn't I ? Sorry. I'll move off, shall I ? I didn't realise I was interrupting something."

" I told you it wasn't the letter."

" Well, something's wrong to-day."

" A bad mood, that's all."

" I'd never have thought you got them."

" Doesn't everybody ? "

He frowned, as if for some reason this was an idea that he did not like to consider. " Do they ? Well, then, why don't you talk about it ? "

" About what ? "

" The mood—or whatever brought it on."

" It wouldn't interest you."

" Well, that's the only thing to do with a mood—unless you think a drink would help. Would you like to go into San Antioco and have a drink ? "

His reddened, freckled face, with the fair hair flopping over it, showed what seemed to be some real concern.

" My moods aren't anything to worry about," Ruth assured him. " They wear off by themselves."

" Well, why not come and have the drink, anyway ? "

He had never suggested anything of the sort before and Ruth caught herself wondering at once what was behind it.

While she hesitated, he went on, " You haven't got to stay at home all day, have you ? Come and have a drink and some lunch and then—then we could go out in a boat. Or we might take a *carozza* and go to Ravento. Aren't there some ruins or something at Ravento ? " He had started to speak with what Ruth thought was a certain hurry and anxiety.

" It'd take us the rest of the day to go to Ravento and back by *carozza*," she said. " Besides, I'm going along to see Mrs. Ranzi after lunch."

" Oh? " He sat up. He gave one of his own bare feet a hard stare.

Ruth suddenly became convinced that somehow he had known of her appointment with Marguerite.

" You've got to go, I suppose ? " he said.

"She's expecting me," Ruth said.

"Yes, of course." He slithered forward on the rock and thrust the foot at which he had stared so hard into the water. "It's interesting that you two should be friends," he said. "I can't see the signs of anything in common between you. But perhaps I'm not very bright about such things." He let himself down into the water. "We'll just have the drink and some lunch, then." With a stroke surprisingly powerful and graceful for such a gangling length of man, he started off across the cove.

Ruth watched him idly, thinking that it must somehow be because of her appointment with Marguerite that he wanted her to have this drink with him. Perhaps he hoped that he might casually attach himself to her and be taken along with her when she went to the Ranzis'. Or perhaps he merely wanted to talk about Marguerite. Probably, Ruth thought, he was the sort of man who needed to build up his ego by talking to one woman about another, and, if he seemed to-day to want her company more than he had since she had introduced him a week or so after he had met her to the Ranzis, this wish was certain to be connected with Marguerite.

However, Ruth had in any case to go down to San Antioco that afternoon, so there was no inconvenience in going to lunch there first, if that was what Stephen wanted. When he swam back to her and, with the same trace of anxiety that Ruth had noticed before, repeated his invitation, she accepted it, only pointing out that she would have to return to the villa first to dress. Stephen nodded and swam away from her again.

Presently they climbed up the cliff-path together. While Ruth went indoors to change, Stephen waited on the terrace, and when she came down again, in a dress of lime-green shan-tung, he was sitting on one of the wicker chairs in the shade of the wistaria-covered trellis. Once more the first thing that she noticed when she saw him was that his hair needed cutting. Irritatedly she thought that there was no need for him to look as sloppy as he did. Even if he was a writer, or whatever he was, his flannels could have been cleaned more often and he need not have worn his shirts for so many days.

Looking up at her as she came towards him, he said,
" How long did you say you've been here ? "

" Four years," Ruth said.

" And what do you actually have to do ? "

" Not nearly enough, these days."

" Don't you like that ? " he asked, apparently astonished.

" Not really," she said.

" Why d'you stay then ? "

" Because I'm in a trap."

" A trap ? " He smiled oddly. " Aren't we all ? But I
wouldn't mind your trap, you know. Four years in this
place. . . . Now I'll have to go home just as soon as my
currency runs out."

" Couldn't you get some more by insisting you have to
stay here to finish that book of yours ? "

" That book ? Oh, yes, that book."

" Isn't it going well, then ? "

He laughed, heaving himself to his feet. " That's one
of those questions it's hard to answer. A book can be going
well when you think it isn't—and *vice versa*."

At that point Ruth came to the conclusion that the book
had never had much existence except in his conversation.

But something else was worrying her, something that
had nothing to do with Stephen. She had the feeling that
there was something that she ought to have remembered
but could not. It was only as they started down the road
together that she realised what it was. It was the man in the
checked shirt with the sprig of bougainvillea in his buttonhole, who had sat on the wall that morning, watching the
house. He was not there any more.

But this should have meant that she need not go on
worrying. Yet it did not, and when she and Stephen reached
the bend in the road between the gate and the garage, she
actually glanced behind her to make sure that the road was
still empty.

She started. The road was not empty now. The man was
back, sitting on the wall, smoking a cigarette. Stephen did
not notice her start and she did not mention the man.

They had drinks at a café in the *piazza* in front of the
church. The *piazza* was crowded, as it seemed to be at all
hours of the day and night. Ruth and Stephen sat at a table

under a striped awning, and drank *cinzano bianco* with ice in it. If it was of Marguerite that Stephen wanted to speak, he certainly approached the subject in a devious manner.

" A trap, you were saying," he said.

" Was I ? "

" A financial trap ? " he asked. " One can generally get out of those if one thinks hard enough."

" No, it's not a financial trap," she said. " It's just that I've let a certain responsibility be thrust on me and though I could drop it to-morrow and walk out, I'd feel bad if I did."

" How bad ? "

She gave him an uncertain look. " Well, I don't know exactly."

" It's damn good sense sometimes to do things that make one feel bad," he said. " It can save a lot of trouble later. Only if it makes one feel too bad—well, then one's stuck."

She thought it over. " I'm stuck."

" Something to do with the Ballards ? "

" Yes." She wished she had not said anything to rouse his curiosity, but it was difficult now to stop. " That letter you saw me trying to write this morning—it was to a friend at home whom I was going to ask to help find me a job. But then I began to think of what it might actually mean if I went." A deep frown had settled on her face as she gazed past him across the busy square, where the traffic, which always behaved as if it were something human instead of mechanical, dodged and darted through the slow-moving crowds in a noisy, excitable ballet.

" Are you in love with Ballard, then ? " Stephen asked.

Her gaze came back to him with a jerk.

" Good heavens, no ! "

" Marguerite says you are."

" Well, considering that this job of mine, which you think is so easy, has consisted mostly of trying to counteract the effect that that man's detestable behaviour has on Nicky, who's basically a nice and quite intelligent boy, but who's had such a rotten start in life that stupid people sometimes accuse him of being mentally deficient, I don't think it's probable, do you ? "

" Except that that's one of the spheres where the laws of probability really don't operate. But this boy Nicky . . ."

" Well ? "

" I'm sorry I said anything about his being deficient."

" Oh, it's the way everyone talks," she said. " Lester himself spreads the story, because he thinks it justifies him in refusing to take any trouble over Nicky."

" So the trap is Nicky and his dependence on you ? "

" Yes."

" What was this bad start he had ? " Stephen asked.

" Oh, the usual sort of thing," she said. " His mother dying when he was about four or five. They lived in England. Then the war broke out and Lester was away in the army and Nicky was pushed into some school or other, then that got too expensive, so he was moved to another and so on. He wouldn't learn to read and he developed those awful rages he's never grown out of. When he started getting used to a place and perhaps fond of somebody there, he always seemed to get shifted. Lester hated to have to spend any money on him and was always looking for a cheaper place which would also take Nicky more completely off his hands. Then when the war was over, Lester discovered that his father-in-law had died and that he'd inherited the family business in Naples, so they came out here. In a way that was another disaster for Nicky, because he's the sort of boy who simply can't learn a foreign language and that's helped to keep him strange and outside of things, because now he doesn't speak proper Italian or proper English."

" And you were brought in to look after him ? "

" Not at first. To begin with there were only the Gargiulos. Madge is English, you know, and I suppose was meant to provide a slight feeling of familiarity in a foreign land. Sometimes I am surprised that Lester was considerate enough to think of even that, still, he did and I think Madge did her best, but she just couldn't cope with Nicky. So that was when I was brought in."

" I've always thought it must have been an unpleasant shock for you, getting here and finding that you'd still got to put up with English cooking. Incidentally, Ballard's quite a bit of a crook, isn't he ? "

With her thoughts still on Nicky and his problems that had become her problems, Ruth took a moment to take in what Stephen had said. " A crook ? "

" Well, I went into Naples last week," he said, " and I wandered round that antique shop of his and it all seemed pretty spurious. Not that swindling the tourist isn't a reasonably legal activity, not excepting in the *Provincia di Napoli*."

" I don't know much about that sort of thing," Ruth said. " I've only been to the shop once or twice. I know it used to have a very good reputation when his father-in-law was alive. In fact, it was quite famous. But tell me "—she returned to the sore point—" did Marguerite *really* tell you I was in love with Lester ? "

" Yes."

" Did she believe it ? Was she serious ? "

" How does one know when Marguerite is serious ? "

" Yes, that's sometimes a problem, isn't it ? "

" You know——" He finished his drink, then started twisting the glass so that the remaining little chunk of ice clinked inside it. " If you really don't like the set-up here, you're stupid to stay."

" But there's Nicky."

" You won't help him much by staying, even if he's worth helping."

" How d'you know ? "

" Because trying to help people never works out the way you want it to."

" Yes, it does, sometimes."

" It doesn't."

She frowned at him. " Well, you have to try, don't you ? "

" You have to try to learn to stop trying—and don't think that's a counsel of pure selfishness."

" What is it, then ? Bitter experience ? "

" No more bitter than most people's," he said equably. " What I'm thinking of are the people who've tried to help me and made a mess of it. There are lots of people you can't help and if you don't try, at least you don't end up with a grudge against them. Now, let's go and eat, shall we ? " He beckoned to the waiter for the bill.

Standing up, Ruth said, " Well, earlier this morning I'd have agreed with you, but when I tried to write that letter, I couldn't. That's all there was to it. I didn't do any reasoning about it, I simply couldn't write the letter."

" And so you're in a trap. And as I said before, how happily I'd change places with you. If only it weren't for Mrs. Gargiulo's Irish stew and steak and kidney pudding."

They had started walking across the *piazza*, turning into a narrow street which was an avenue of blossoming oleanders.

" As a matter of fact, Madge's cooking is marvellous and completely Italian," Ruth said. " I think Cesare must have taught her before he decided to give up all forms of work for the rest of his life. He still drives the car and potters down the road to buy wine for the household, but with him those things come under the heading of pleasure rather than work. Stephen——"

" Yes ? "

" How much longer are you staying here in San Antioco ? "

" Only another week or two," he said. " It's taken me quite a bit of wangling to stay even as long as I have. Perhaps I could wangle some more if I gave my mind to it, but I'm not sure. . . ." He stopped in front of the doorway of a small restaurant and gestured at it questioningly.

Ruth nodded and stepped inside. Through another doorway at the end of a narrow, dark room, full of the rich smell of food, they could see tables laid with white cloths in a shady garden. A waiter came forward and led them to one of the tables.

" So you wouldn't necessarily stay longer even if you could ? " Ruth asked as they sat down. " You wouldn't really jump at my job if it was offered to you ? "

" Oh, if it was *offered* to me. . . . Having something handed to you on a plate is rather different from going scrounging after it. But no one's going to offer it to me and I couldn't really claim to be qualified for it, either. Your good intentions by that child Nicky move me to deep admiration, but if I had to put up with him for a week, he'd drive me nuts. Now what shall we eat ? "

It was spoken perfectly pleasantly and yet it left Ruth with an uneasy feeling that Stephen thought there was something the matter with her because Nicky did not drive her nuts.

She had never been made to feel this by anyone else before. She had always been rather sure that a superior insight and power of sympathy had made her able to see in

Nicky, at least whenever she had had him to herself, a likeable and interesting boy. But now, quite suddenly, Stephen had imparted to her a puzzling misgiving. Had she somewhere made a serious mistake about her own attitude? Would a reasonably strong-minded person have gone on writing the letter that she had abandoned? Was the trap of which she had been complaining simply of her own making? Or rather, was it not a trap at all, but a refuge?

She began to feel sure, even though he had said nothing of the sort, that this was what Stephen had meant. Her good intentions by Nicky, she thought, had not really moved him to admiration of any kind, but only to a mild sort of contempt. Very mild, of course. Most of Stephen's feelings would be rather mild and vague. He had not really a great deal of self-confidence himself, though he was as anxious as most people not to have this found out. So, come to think of it, he had no real right to criticise her, or Nicky, either. He was not a person who showed the signs of having made much success of his life. He must be at least thirty, yet he seemed still to be drifting in a rather depressed and fretful fashion, not even getting much pleasure out of his idleness. No doubt, if one questioned him, he would blame it all on the war, though if one pointed out that other people had been through the war without having arrived at the same point, he would immediately agree with one. He was the kind of person who always admitted the truth of any accusations made against him, thinking that by the admission he had disposed of the whole matter. In fact, not a very impressive character. And on top of everything, he was unable to acquire a respectable tan and he needed a haircut.

Having arrived at this point, Ruth had convinced herself that the antagonism that she had felt towards Stephen Evers, almost from the first, was justified. However, for some reason best known to himself, Stephen had done what he could to be pleasant to her that morning and had not merely seized the chance to talk about Marguerite Ranzi. Acknowledging this, Ruth in return was as pleasant as she was able to be. But she kept reminding herself that the meal was not yet over and that some object for the invitation might still appear.

But no object did appear, none, that is, that she could possibly have recognised at the time.

He mentioned Marguerite only once more. It was when they were outside again in the street and just as they were about to separate. " So you're going straight along to the Ranzi's place now, are you ? " he said.

" Yes," Ruth said.

" Will you be staying long ? " But as soon as he had asked this, he looked annoyed with himself, as if the question had slipped out without his having intended it. Before Ruth could answer, he went on, " I think I'll go back to my pub and have a sleep."

" Pleasant dreams," Ruth said.

" I never have them," he answered. " All my dreams are quite stupid and pointless. Well, give my love to Marguerite."

" I will," Ruth said.

They started walking away from each other, Stephen back towards the *piazza* and Ruth in the opposite direction, towards the villa of the Ranzis.

III

RUTH DID NOT keep the promise that she had just given to Stephen. There was a simple reason for this. When she reached the Ranzis' villa, Marguerite was not there. Nor was her husband, Amedeo. Nor was their maid.

But the door stood wide open, as if someone had just gone out and would be returning in a few minutes, so Ruth decided to go in and wait.

The Ranzis' villa was big, with a slightly shabby air of grandeur about it. Its marble staircase was wide, with a gilded handrail. Its rooms were lofty, with painted ceilings, mosaic floors, sombre, imposing furniture and lights concealed in swirls of delicate glass. In the garden a fountain played in a carved marble basin, the water sparkling above the figure of a small, crouching faun. Yet the place did not give an impression of real wealth. Though Amedeo Ranzi had once been a rich importer of colonial products, with big offices in Naples, he had lost a good deal of his business during the war, and in order to provide ready money, many of the more valuable objects that had once been in the house had been sold. Lester Ballard had handled most of the sales for him, with results apparently very satisfactory to the Ranzis, for Ballard was on terms of close friendship with them.

Ruth went into the drawing-room to wait for Marguerite. The walk to the villa had been very hot and it was agreeable to sit in the big, shuttered room, listening to the rippling sound of the fountain outside. There was a vase of canna lilies on the table and beside it some sewing of Marguerite's, scattered there as if it had been put down only for a moment. Certain that she would be back soon, Ruth settled herself on a low, brocade-covered couch near the window.

The dimness and quiet of the room, after the heat outside, brought on a drowsiness that made her forget the time. It felt quite natural to be sitting there peacefully without the hostess who had rung her up that morning on purpose to urge her to come early. Ruth had been waiting there for nearly half an hour before, coming to herself with a start, it occurred to her to wonder what had really happened to Marguerite.

After that she rapidly became restless, while the minutes passed with increasing slowness. Marguerite's absence now began to seem very strange, annoying and even disturbing. She was often casual and unpunctual but had never before done anything quite like this. There must, Ruth thought, be some peculiar reason for it.

Uncertain whether or not to stay any longer, she started to walk about the room. It was only then that she noticed what she might have seen on coming into the room if the sudden change from the brilliant light outside to the shadows of the room had not made her unable to distinguish much inside it. On the table, propped against the base of the vase of canna lilies, was a note. It was to her. It said, " Ever so sorry to have had to dash out. Back soon. Do wait. Marguerite."

So she had been right to wait, though the note did not happen to mention how long she was expected to stay there. Picking up a book, Ruth went back to the couch and sat down again. But she had become impatient and found waiting more difficult. At the end of another half-hour, she became too exasperated to stay any longer and started home. Before leaving she wrote a few words at the bottom of the note that Marguerite had left for her. " Sorry, can't wait any longer."

Outside, the heat was still as intense as when she had arrived. The whiteness of the dusty road was almost blinding. She had not brought her sun-glasses and her head was uncovered. As she screwed up her eyes against the glare, she realised that she had the beginnings of a headache. But when a *carozza* driver, coming down the hill towards her as she came out of the house, turned his vehicle in the road and drove along beside her, urging her to let him drive her home, she replied, " No thank you, Giulio."

He went on driving beside her. He was a gaunt old man with a thin, hawk-nosed face in which there was a blending of an almost piratical fierceness and a mild and dignified innocence.

" Very cheap," he coaxed her. " I take you up to the villa for very little. Only three hundred lire, signorina."

But Ruth had brought only a little money with her and in any case hardly ever treated herself to this luxury. " No, thank you," she repeated.

He began to reason with her. " Too hot to walk now. Two hundred. I take you up for two hundred."

When she still shook her head, he said, " Well, then, you give me what you like, I leave it to you."

When even this was unsuccessful, raising his ancient, green pork-pie hat in a flourish, he gave up and drove away.

As Ruth walked on, her headache grew worse. But luckily, she knew, there was some aspirin in her room and the house would still be empty, so that she would have time to deal with the headache before anyone started wanting her attention. As she walked, she found herself worrying increasingly over what could have happened to Marguerite. So far Ruth had not become really annoyed with Marguerite, but had assumed that something unexpected and important must have occurred, so that she had not been able to help her absence. But on reaching the corner by the village shop, where the cliff-path turned off from the road, Ruth suddenly became very angry.

A car was parked there, a small Fiat, and the car was Marguerite's.

So Marguerite had simply decided that in spite of her invitation, she must have a swim and having driven up here, vaguely meaning, perhaps, to be back in time, had found the water so pleasant, or else had met someone she so much wanted to talk to, that she had simply not troubled to return. In a much worse temper, Ruth went on to the gate of the villa and went up to her room.

Her bedroom was full of flies. They circled around her, descending on her to taste her heated skin. Waving them irritatedly away, she looked for the aspirins. As she did so, she found that she was holding something in her hand. It was a box of matches. For a moment she could not think how it could possibly have got into her hand, then she remembered that a moment before, in crossing the terrace to the house, she had noticed the box of matches lying on the table. She supposed that she had picked it up automatically.

Dropping it on her dressing-table, she shook a couple of aspirins out of the bottle and swallowed them. Then she lay down on the bed and closed her eyes. Her anger against Marguerite soon faded in a new wave of drowsiness. If the friendship between the two of them had been closer, Ruth might have been angry for longer or else not angry at all, but as it was she was never inclined to let her thoughts dwell on Marguerite, either in anger or in affection, for very long at a time.

The flies went on bothering Ruth and prevented her from falling quite asleep. But the sharpness of her headache soon passed, leaving only a dull discomfort. Presently she found herself thinking again about the morning's quarrel. She thought about the fact that perhaps there would be another quarrel, as bad as this morning's had been, or an even worse one, the next day. Or if not the next day, then the day after. And one day the situation really would become intolerable.

She thought about the fact that after all, although she had tried so hard, she had not succeeded in doing a great deal for Nicky. She had not had the right sort of knowledge with which to approach her task. Nicky was still a bad misfit. Most people thought him unbearable and that morning she herself had actually felt fear of him. So why should she stay?

At that point she got up to have a drink of water. As she did so, she heard a door either opening or closing somewhere downstairs. This surprised her for she had not expected anyone to have come home yet. But it did not seem necessary for her to investigate the sound and when she had had a drink, she went back to the bed. Yet, after a minute or two, she began to think that the sound must have been made by Nicky, that he must have come back from his tutor earlier than usual and that this probably meant trouble of some sort. Reluctantly she got up again and went out on to the landing.

She could see into the hall and she could see that the door of the drawing-room was open. But whether or not it had been open earlier she could not be sure. There was no sound of anyone moving about. Nicky, however, generally wore rope-soled sandals, in which he walked noiselessly on the tiled floors.

She waited for a moment, then she called, questioningly, " Nicky ? "

At the sound, someone shot out of the drawing-room, across the hall and out by the front door. It was such a strange-looking figure that for an instant she hardly recognised it. Yet it was Nicky. It was Nicky, slim, dark and handsome, but with his face distorted into a grimace of a kind that she had never seen before and with his cheeks, his hands and his shirt dabbled with what looked like red paint. He was carrying something in one hand, but he was gone before Ruth could see what it was.

She raced down the stairs, calling out to him to wait. By the time that she had reached the door, he had disappeared. Running out on to the terrace and craning over the wall, she caught a glimpse of him on his bicycle, swooping madly down the road towards San Antioco. In an instant he was out of sight.

With a sick feeling in her throat, Ruth went slowly back into the house. Nicky's face had been a terrifying sight. Emotion of extreme violence had dragged it all out of shape, while the red smears had turned it into something conceived in a nightmare. Yet, in the way of nightmares, there was a curious familiarity about it. It was as if Ruth had always known that Nicky could look like that. It was as if she had always known that, sooner or later, this was how she would see him.

Walking stiffly, dreading to take each step, she went to the drawing-room. No sense of familiarity came this time. Pure shock sent an ice-cold wave through her body. There was a moment of blackness, when she had no consciousness, then she found herself fighting the need to be sick. She was trembling all over and she could not make herself take another step into the room.

Lester Ballard lay there, dead. He was horribly dead, his head a broken pulp of blood and bone. He was in a corner of the room, as if he had been driven there before he was struck down. Blood lay in a puddle and spattered the tiled floor near him. Blood was thick and dark on his clothes. The hot, shady room smelt of blood and already it was full of flies, wheeling and droning in the shuttered twilight.

There were not many signs of a struggle. A small table had been overturned. A silver vase, containing some sprays of pink geraniums, had fallen to the floor and lay beside the body. Nicky must have taken his father unawares or have proved to be much stronger than he, so that Ballard had been cowed and overpowered at once. He had been a small, slight man and he had always had a look of brittleness about him, which in life had gone with a kind of animated, bird-like elegance but which now helped to give him the look of a trampled insect.

At last Ruth went farther into the room. She walked almost up to the body and, while the room swam round her again, forced herself to look at the unrecognisable face. Her own face was almost unrecognisable as she did so, but she did not know that.

Something made her stoop and pick up the silver vase. Setting it down in its usual place on a walnut cabinet against the wall, she started to straighten the flowers. But as she did so, she realised that in touching the vase her hands had become slimy with blood. She withdrew them sharply and the vase toppled. It fell on to the tiled floor with a clang. The pink geraniums, tumbling out of the vase, scattered themselves on the floor. Their petals became tipped with red.

Ruth stood looking at her hands. Instinctively, she had been about to brush them against her dress, but had stopped herself just in time. Holding them out before her, she stared at them incredulously as if she had no knowledge of how the blood had come to be smeared on her palms.

As she stared, a voice asked quietly, " Why did you do it ? "

IV

IT WAS Stephen Evers. He was standing in the doorway, looking almost as sick as Ruth, though his eyes were steadier. Their gaze was hard and bright. Yet there was a shadow of utter bewilderment behind them.

Ruth let her hands fall to her sides but remembered to hold them away from her skirt.

" What are you doing here ? " she asked. Her voice came in a dry whisper.

Stephen came farther into the room. The mere sight of a dead body did not seem to affect him as violently as it did Ruth, yet she realised, as he came closer to her, that he, too, was trembling.

He repeated hoarsely, " Why ? "

" But I didn't . . ."

Perhaps he did not hear her, for he went on, " What had he been doing ? "

" I don't know."

" I didn't guess . . . I didn't realise . . ." The steadiness of his gaze wavered and dissolved into a look of hopeless confusion.

Ruth repeated her own question more excitably, " What are you doing here ? When did you come ? "

" Just now," he said.

" How did you get in ? "

" I walked in. Everything was open. I heard a noise."

" The vase falling over."

" Oh, the vase."

Like Ruth, he stooped and reached for it, but she caught his arm and pulled it back.

" Don't—you'll get blood on you ! "

Straightening, he looked down at her hands that clutched at his sleeve. She drew them back with a jerk. The white cotton of his sleeve was stained with red.

Deliberately, though his hands were still shaking, he started to roll his sleeves up above the elbow, so that the stains disappeared in the folds.

" You'd better go and wash your hands," he said.

As if she had been waiting for someone to tell her what to do, she started towards the door, but after only a couple of steps she stopped and turned, staring at him blankly.

" What am I to do ? " she asked.

" Tell me what happened," he said more insistently.

" I don't know. I heard a noise. I came out and . . ." Her next word would have been ' Nicky,' but before she could speak the name, her voice dried up in her throat.

He was looking round now.

" Wait a minute," he said. " Are you alone here ? "

" Yes."

" Where's everyone else ? "

" The Gargiulos went into Naples with—with Lester this morning."

" He went into Naples, did he ? "

" Yes."

" When did he get back ? "

" I don't know. I didn't know he was back."

" And where's the boy ? "

" Nicky ? " She managed to say the name this time, but before she could go on again, she had to draw a long breath. " At his tutor's, I suppose. . . . Where are you going ? " She asked this sharply as Stephen walked quickly out of the room.

He did not reply, and in a panic, she followed him. He crossed the hall, closed the door that opened on to the terrace and slid the bolts.

" What's the good of doing that ? " she asked.

" Give us time to think. We don't want anyone else barging in."

" Like you did ? "

"Yes." He missed the real meaning of what she said. "How long before the Gargiulos come back?"

"A long time still. Midnight, perhaps."

"And Nicky?"

"I—don't know."

He walked back into the drawing-room. He did not go so near the dead body this time, but stayed in the middle of the room, looking round it searchingly with his bright, concentrated yet inwardly bewildered, glance.

"All right, go on now and tell me what happened," he said.

She had a feeling that she would start crying at any moment. Pure shock had helped to prevent it till then, but now she could feel the pressure of tears choking her. Slowly, carefully, she said, "I don't know what happened. I was upstairs. I heard a noise. I came down and found . . . What are you looking for?" For with a deep frown, Stephen had begun to wander about the room, obviously searching for some particular thing.

"Matches." Out in the hall he had stuck a cigarette between his lips but it was still unlit. "I had some but I seem to have left them somewhere. Oh . . . sorry." It had only just occurred to him that she might like a cigarette, too. He held out a packet.

She reached for one, but then withdrew her hand.

"I'll wash these first. And I'll bring some matches." She went out to the kitchen.

She took some time to wash her hands. Something made her let the water from the tap flow over them far longer than was necessary. While the water flowed, she tried to force her mind into a state in which she could begin to think. But she could only think of danger. Not any particular danger, from any particular source or in any particular form, but simply danger in the air, in the shadows of the house, in the sunlight outside, in the roar of a motor-cycle passing, in the silence after it.

When she returned to the drawing-room, Stephen took a look at her and said, "You'd better give yourself a drink, you know. What have you got in the place? Brandy?"

"No, thanks." She handed him the matches that she had brought from the kitchen.

"Then, for pity's sake, get me some," he said.

She did not move to do so, but stood looking earnestly and curiously into his face.

"You haven't telephoned the police yet," she said. She was deeply puzzled by this, and in some way it contributed to her fear. There was something not normal about it, something that did not belong to the pattern of things that she understood.

"No," he said, frowning and turning away from her.

"When are you going to?"

"Let's have a drink and think this thing over. You've got to tell me what happened."

Her voice slipped into shrillness. "I've told you, I don't know what happened."

"Listen, if you want me to help you . . ." He stopped. He seemed all at once to become violently angry. "Are you going to get that drink or not? D'you think we've got all day? Don't you understand anything might happen at any moment?"

Silently she went to the cabinet where Lester Ballard had kept his brandy. There was a decanter there, nearly full. She took it out, with a glass for Stephen. Then she took out a second glass and filled them both.

As she handed one glass to Stephen, she said, "You don't have to help me."

"I know I don't." He drank. "Now go on and talk—quickly."

"But I've told you everything I know already. I was upstairs in my room. I heard a noise——"

"For God's sake!" He was so tense that she saw he could scarcely get the words out. "Don't be a fool. Talk to me. Tell me what really happened, then if I can, I'll help you."

"What can you do?"

"I don't know. Nothing—nothing unless you tell me what really happened!"

She put her glass down. She did not feel that the brandy would steady her, but only that it would let out of her the tears and the terror that she was feverishly trying to contain.

"You think I did it," she said. "I know it looks like it. But I didn't."

" Who did then ? "

" I don't know." The words shot out quickly.

" D'you want me to believe that this could happen in here without your hearing anything ? "

" I was upstairs. I was half dopey. I'd taken some aspirins and lain down. When I got back from Marguerite's I'd a furious headache, so I went straight upstairs and I nearly went to sleep. Perhaps I did go to sleep. And then I heard a noise."

" What kind of noise ? "

" A door being opened—or closed. I don't know which."

" Did you have a nice time with Marguerite ? "

The question made her start. It was so pointless, yet it was not asked idly but with a staring look of antagonism.

" As a matter of fact, I didn't see her," she replied. " She wasn't there."

" How strange," he said. " How very strange."

" Yes, it *was* strange." She was fiercely resentful at his tone. " She rang me up this morning on purpose to remind me that she was expecting me and then she went off swimming. Still, that's not important."

" No ? You really did go to her house, I suppose ? "

" Of course I went to her house."

" Who saw you ? "

" At the house ? No one. It was empty."

He rubbed a hand across his forehead. The look of confusion had returned. He muttered, " It isn't much of a story. We *will* have to think. Perhaps we can do better. Now, listen——"

" Listen to me," she said. " Everything I've told you is true. I went to the Ranzis, just as I said. There was no one about, but there was a note there, asking me to wait. So I waited for about an hour. Then I came back here. I went up to my room and I took some aspirin and lay down. And I didn't hear anything except a door closing. When I heard that, I came down here to see who it was, but I didn't see anyone. I came in here and I found—him. And that was only a few minutes before you walked in. And you still haven't told me what you're doing here."

" At the minute, trying to think," he said. " Just trying to think."

"If you don't believe me," she said, "will you tell me what I killed him with? And what have I done with the weapon?"

"Strange to say, that's one of the things I've been trying to think about," he said. Emptying his glass, he put it down, walked over to the body, bent and picked up the silver vase. "Too light," he said and let it drop again. But he remained stooping, the repugnance in his face altering suddenly to sharp surprise. "Ruth, there's something queer here, isn't there? It's only just struck me. Come and look."

Ruth came only a step or two nearer. She did not look. "What is it?" she asked.

"His clothes. Ballard liked silk suits, didn't he? And expensive shoes and so on. Then what's he dressed like this for?"

As soon as he had said it, Ruth could not imagine how she had managed not to become aware till then that Lester Ballard was wearing clothes in which she had never seen him before. He was wearing a suit of tan gaberdine, obviously cheap and new, a green cotton shirt, a tie with a staring pattern of palm trees and a sunset on it, and pointed brown suède shoes that looked as if they could not possibly have cost more than two thousand *lire*.

It was fantastic. That Lester, always vain about his clothes, passionately fussy about fine textures and good tailoring, loving to be noticeable but only in the restrained taste suitable to real opulence, should be found masquerading, in death, in those shoddy, flashy clothes, was unbelievable. It was almost as unbelievable as that he should be dead, that he should be murdered.

In her interest, Ruth had come closer.

"And his watch!" she exclaimed. "Look at his watch!" For the watch on his thin wrist, protruding from the loose, brown gaberdine sleeve, was of chromium, on a leather strap, instead of the watch that he usually wore, which was of gold, on a bracelet of gold links.

"Does it make any sense to you?" Stephen asked.

She shook her head. "It just isn't like him. He wouldn't be seen dead in these clothes."

Stephen laughed shortly. "His death appears to have been involuntary. He didn't mean to be seen dead in

them. He meant something else. I scent a double life.
And I suppose you don't know anything about that
either." He had straightened up and was looking into
her face again with his hard, bright stare that suggested in
some way that he had a personal grudge against her. His
look was not one of horror, such as he might comprehensibly
have turned on a murderess, but rather something more
secret, more intimate, more unreadable.

She heard herself saying, " Don't look at me like that.
I don't like it."

To her surprise, he immediately dropped his eyes.

" The next question is," he said, " how did he get here ?
There's no car outside."

" He left by car this morning," Ruth said. " He drove
off to the station as usual. He'd have parked the car there
and taken the train into Naples. The car's probably at the
station, still."

" Mightn't it be in the garage ? "

" I've never known Lester bother to put the car into the
garage in his life. He always left that for Gargiulo to do.
I think someone else must have driven him home."

" So there's no car here now," Stephen said thoughtfully.
" That's a pity."

" Why is it a pity ? "

" Because without any car, it's going to be a bit difficult
disposing of the body, isn't it ? "

For a moment the words sounded quite reasonable to
Ruth. She had been saying something like them to herself
for some minutes. Without any car, it would be very difficult
to move Lester Ballard's body away from the house. Then
suddenly she realised how astounding it was that the words
should have been spoken by Stephen.

" But you don't mean that you . . ." She stopped, for
it was quite clear from the look on Stephen's face, that he
did mean it.

He was considering the body again with a calculating
expression, as if he were trying to guess its weight.

" Only we'll have to get a car," he said. For no apparent
reason his voice had dropped to a whisper. " We'll have
to get a car somehow, but it might be best to wait till after
dark. You're sure the Gargiulos won't walk in on us ? "

" I don't think they will. But we can't do this, Stephen. You can't do it. I won't let you."

" Got any better ideas ? "

" The police . . ."

" You want to go to the police with that story of yours ? "

" Why not ? " But her heart began to thump in a sickening way. " Anyway, you mustn't get mixed up in it. It's not your affair. I won't let you."

" Noble of you. And pretty noble of me, too, sticking around. Now that's been said. We're two very, very fine people in an awkward situation. And we still need a car. I wonder now. . . ."

An idea had occurred to him. But Ruth never found out what it was, for at that moment someone knocked on the front door.

It was a moment of sheer terror.

Instinctively Ruth and Stephen moved together. She felt his shoulder pressing hers. Then the knock came again.

" Who is it ? " he asked in her ear.

" I don't know."

" Not at all ? "

" No."

" They may have heard us from the window. They may know we're here."

" But I can't go and open it ! "

" I think you'd better."

Turning her head swiftly, she looked at him disbelievingly.

" Go on," he whispered, giving her shoulder a push. " Go on and get rid of whoever it is."

" But suppose I can't ? "

" You've got to somehow."

" Suppose I can't and they come in ? They'll find you here."

His glance flicked towards the window. " Yes," he said. " But go on, risk it."

Though her mind was full of doubts, she yielded to his decision, more quickly formed than hers. But she had no faith in it. When she walked towards the front door, Stephen went with her as far as the door of the sitting-room, and as soon as she had passed through it, closed it behind her.

Alone in the hall, Ruth went forward and opened the door on to the terrace. Facing her were two policemen.

Both of them were young men, in grey-green uniforms. One had a round, plump face, a peasant's face, grey-eyed and boyish. The other's was thin and brown, with long, black lashes curling back from luminous dark eyes. It was the dark one who asked, " Signora Ballard ? "

" No," Ruth replied in her stiff Italian, " there is no Signora Ballard. Whom do you wish to see ? "

" We wish——" The man hesitated. Though Ruth was looking at him through a mist of apprehension, she realised that his manner was gentle, in fact, even concerned. " We have some bad news, I fear. It concerns Signor Ballard. You are a relation ? "

" No," Ruth replied, " I am employed here. Has—has something happened to Signor Ballard ? "

She heard herself ask this question with complete amazement at her own ability to speak such words. But the *agente's* reply blotted out all thought of what she had said.

" Yes, we are very sorry to have to inform you that the body of Signor Ballard has been found about two kilometres from here on the road into the mountains. He appears to have been knocked down and run over by a car. He must have been killed instantly. We are very deeply distressed that——"

He got no further. At that moment, the two young men with their earnestly sympathetic faces, the sunlit terrace, the mountains and the shining blue sea were swallowed in blackness. Unconscious, Ruth slid to the floor.

V

SHE BECAME conscious again abruptly, with her mind sharp and clear. Or so it felt. Yet she could not make out where she was. She was lying on a couch, but the glimpse that she had about her, as her eyelids flickered up, did not make sense. However, as she lay there, now deliberately keeping her eyes shut and thinking of that glimpse that she had had, she realised what had happened. She was back in the drawing-room. She was lying on the green and white striped couch that stood against the wall under the window. Only it was not under the window any more. It was in a corner of the room, almost facing the window.

The shutters had been opened and the window showed a rectangle of the bright sky, edged with glowing sprays of bougainvillea. So Stephen had gone. That glance of his towards the window, as he and she had stood arguing whether or not she should go to the door, had told her his intention. For some reason, this hurt badly. It was not that she had had any reason to expect him to stand by her, but all the same, there was treachery in going like that, without warning, by the window.

Then she heard Stephen saying, "There, that's better. But take things easily. Don't try to talk yet."

So he had not gone after all and his words, spoken in the calm tone of one who reassured a person taken suddenly ill, contained an urgent warning to her to keep silence.

She waited another moment after hearing him speak, then opened her eyes again. She could not see him at first, because he was standing behind her, at the head of the couch. But she saw the two policemen, looking down at her with expressions of concern. This was not the expression that she had expected to see on the faces of policemen who had just discovered a woman in a house together with a corpse that had been violently battered to death. In fact, when she had opened her eyes, the two men had even smiled at her and then at one another, as if congratulating themselves on her rapid recovery.

She began to have a hazy, foolish feeling that everything was perfectly all right. She had been having a bad dream, she had waked suddenly and everyone was being kind to her, telling her not to be frightened. But as she took in what must actually have occurred during the time that she had been unconscious, this feeling passed in a flash. The same sense of prickling cold that she had felt on first seeing the dead body, spread through her.

Stephen must have seen some change in her face at that moment, for his hand came down on her shoulder.

" Now, don't worry, you're quite all right," he said. " It was just the shock. You fainted. These two gentlemen understand perfectly and they want you to take your time before you start to answer some questions they want to ask you."

Though he spoke in English, it was apparent that the two policemen understood the drift of what he was saying, for they both nodded their heads animatedly. This was another warning to Ruth to be careful of what she said in English as well as in Italian.

But Ruth's mind really had cleared by now and the warning was unnecessary. She knew that the body of Lester Ballard was behind the couch on which she was lying. She knew that the moment that she had left the room to answer the knocking at the door, Stephen must have grabbed the big, heavy couch and pushed it across the room to the corner where it now stood, concealing the body. He had not relied on her being able to get rid of whoever was at the door. He had acted with swift, crazy resourcefulness and so far, at least, with success.

Ruth felt speechless with gratitude. But this action of his had committed her, whether she wished it or not, to following his counsel. There was no question now of telling the police how she had found the body. She would have to join with Stephen, if he really meant to go on helping her, in getting rid of it.

Trying not to let the lawlessness of the action appal her too hopelessly, she sat up and said, " I'm quite all right now. Please go ahead and ask me what you want to."

The dark-haired *maresciallo* said, " It is a question of identification. It is customary in such cases to ask the nearest relative of the deceased to make a formal identification of the body. Would the *signorina* please be so good as to tell us the name of the nearest relative of Signor Ballard ? "

" It's his son," Ruth said, " a young boy."

" A child ? Has he no other relative ? "

" None that I know of."

" This boy then, how old is he ? "

" Sixteen. And he's a very nervous child, easily upset. If I could go instead. . . ." She hesitated, not knowing how she would be able to face it a second time, yet thinking of Nicky fleeing on his bicycle, wondering where he could have got to by now.

The two men consulted together for a moment, then the dark one went on, " It would perhaps be best, though we regret that the *signorina* should have to perform such an unpleasant task. But it will be over in a moment."

" Then is he very . . . ? "

" Yes, I am afraid so. The road up there is stony and it appears to have been a heavy vehicle that passed over him."

" In that case——" She had been wanting to ask this question so badly that her throat dried up in the middle of it and she had to clear it and start again. " In that case, how do you know that this dead man is Signor Ballard ? "

" There are documents in his pockets that reveal his identity."

" There—there couldn't be some mistake ? "

The man shrugged. " It is possible. But I myself know Signor Ballard by sight and I am afraid—I am sorry— that it is he."

" I'll come with you, then."

" Please, not unless you are quite recovered."

" I'm quite all right, thank you. I'm sorry I was so stupid just now."

Beside her, Stephen mumbled, " Damn it, where are those matches ? Why can't I keep hold of a box of matches ? "

He had an unlit cigarette between his lips and was looking around him in nervous desperation. Looking at him properly for the first time since she had regained consciousness, Ruth was struck by how haggard his face had become. His voice, soothing her and warning her, had been so calm that the sight of his pale, agitated face gave her a great surprise.

"There," she said, pointing to where the box of matches that she had fetched for him earlier lay on a table. She thought, as she did so, "He's scared to death."

Stephen plunged across the room as if the matches were vital to his survival over the next few moments, and drew feverishly on the cigarette. But again his voice was level when he spoke. "Perhaps, Signor Maresciallo, I should accompany the *signorina*. If I could help . . ." He paused questioningly, looking not at the young police officer, but at Ruth.

Speaking as evenly, Ruth said, "Thank you so much, but I'll be quite all right with these gentlemen. You've already been very kind, Stephen. You've helped me so much and I'm deeply grateful."

"You can count on me at any time," Stephen said gravely, "to do anything possible to help you."

"Thank you," she said again. "Then I'll see you later?"

"Of course."

It was as much as they could arrange at that moment.

"If you should see Nicky . . ." Ruth began, but she did not finish. She did not know what to ask Stephen to do if Nicky should come back.

"Don't worry," he said. "I'll look after him."

She turned to the others. "Then let's go."

"Good," the *maresciallo* said. "As I said, I am very sorry to have to ask you to perform this unpleasant duty, but you will see, it will soon be over. It will be quite easy."

He was right in this. It was easy. It was much too easy.

During the drive into San Antioco, Ruth tried to think. But her mind, dazed by shock, could only take in visual things, like the group of women seated at the edge of the road, waiting for the water-cart to come up the hill from the town. The fat old woman from the shop was in the midst of the group. Ruth went on thinking about the dark, animated faces of the women by the roadside when she ought to have been struggling with her unspeakable problem.

If she had been able to think, if she had had the chance of consultation with Stephen, and if she had had the faintest understanding of how it was possible for Lester Ballard to be violently dead in two places at the same time, she might have done other than she did when, in the morgue, the sheet was drawn back from the body of a man and a voice said to her questioningly, " Well ? "

She might have said that she had never seen this man before, or that she was not sure, or that she did not know. But instead, shutting her eyes tight after one brief look, she nodded her head. The sheet was replaced.

The *maresciallo* who had stayed close to her, showing that if she should faint again he was prepared, and indeed willing, to have her limp body collapse in his arms, led her out, taking her into an office where another man in uniform, senior to the others, in fact, the *Commissario* himself insisted on her drinking a glass of wine, then asked her to make a formal statement that the dead man she had just seen was Lester Ballard.

The *Commissario* was a very big man, some inches over six feet and broad and heavy. His hair was thin and grey. He had a bald, rounded forehead, beetling grey eyebrows and grey, good-humoured eyes.

Afterwards he asked her a number of further questions. Most of them were simple to answer, referring to Lester Ballard's full name, his address, his place of business, his age, and the name and addresses of his relatives in England, if any.

To the last of these questions she replied that she believed that Lester Ballard had relatives in England, since he had claimed to be the younger son of a family of some distinction, but that he had never spoken in detail about it and she was not even sure which part of the country he had come from.

The *Commissario* made notes of all her answers, then asked, " Now, can you tell me this ? What was Signor Ballard doing on the mountain road this afternoon ? Do you know anything about that ? "

She thought for a moment, then said slowly, " No—I don't think so. Not this afternoon."

" Did you know he had gone there ? "

" No, I thought he was in Naples for the day."

" Then did he not come back to his home before setting off up that road ? "

" I don't know. He may have done. But I was out

myself from about half-past twelve until at least four o'clock, or perhaps even later."

"And you have no idea why he should have gone walking up that road in the heat of the day?"

She frowned, shaking her head. "It *is* queer, that he went up there during the afternoon, when it was so hot, though he did go up there quite often in the evening."

"He did? But for what purpose?"

"Simply that he liked to walk, I think. He used to say he had to have some exercise or he'd get fat, and he didn't care for swimming. And there's very little traffic on that road and there's a view from there that he was particularly fond of. It's at a place where there's a small shrine in the rock beside the road. Is that where he was found?"

The *Commissario* nodded. "Only not in the road."

"Not? But I thought . . ."

"Oh, yes, he was killed in the road. There are the tracks in the dust there. But after he had been knocked down and run over, the driver must have stopped and—forgive me, it is horrible—he must have thrown Signor Ballard's body over the wall."

Ruth leant her head on her hands, partly because her head was swimming and partly because she was trying to remember the bend in the mountain road where the shrine was. "But isn't there a sheer precipice there? Doesn't it drop straight down into a ravine with a stream at the bottom? In that case, how did you find him?"

"The precipice isn't quite sheer," the *Commissario* said. "There's a cleft with some trees growing out of it. Signor Ballard's body had caught in the trees. A piece of bad luck for the murdering swine."

"The . . .?"

He shrugged his broad shoulders. "These people are like murderers, *signorina*. Sometimes I think they are worse. But now, please, will you look at these?" Opening a cupboard, he took out a bundle and laid it on the table in front of Ruth. "You recognise these things, do you?"

The bundle consisted of a silk suit, badly torn and stained with blood and dust, a silk shirt, a pair of silk socks, a pair of shoes, a gold watch on a gold bracelet, a gold cigarette-case, a pigskin wallet, some keys on a key-ring, a fountain pen and a few of the miscellaneous objects that collect in the pockets of any man, even one as neat and as vain about his appearance as Lester Ballard.

Speaking the truth this time, Ruth said, " Yes, these are all Signor Ballard's."

The *Commissario* opened the wallet, showing her what was inside it.

" There are at least fifty thousand *lire* here," he said, " so whoever did this thing had no thought of robbery. Even if he was afraid of taking the watch and the cigarettee-case because they might be recognised when he tried to dispose of them, it would have been very easy for him to help himself to this money. But he acted, I suppose, simply in irresponsible madness and fear."

" Do you think you will find him ? " Ruth asked.

" It is possible. Not many cars pass up that road and someone may have noticed the number, or the make of the car, or the appearance of some driver. Yes, it is quite possible. Whatever we do find out, we shall of course communicate to you."

" There'll be an inquest ? "

" Certainly."

" Shall I be wanted ? "

" Probably, I am afraid. But we shall try to make things as easy for you as possible. We'll let you know the arrangements shortly."

That was all, except for a few more polite words of condolence and thanks for her assistance, then the same two men who had fetched her drove her back to the villa.

The place was silent and appeared to be empty when she reached it. Yet it seemed changed. The brightness of the day had gone, the short dusk had already begun and an eeriness that Ruth had never felt there before had invaded the house. In twenty minutes or so the darkness would be complete. For the first time, the thought of that quick transition from light to darkness, instead of an hour or so of lingering twilight in which to grow accustomed to the thought of the night, scared her. She did not dare turn on any lights for fear of what might be seen from outside through chinks in the shutters, yet the shadows seemed to have that living, menacing quality that they can assume for one whose mind is already full of fear.

Ruth had vaguely been expecting that she would find Stephen still here, waiting for her, but since the sound of her arrival had not brought him to meet her, she guessed that he had gone. She felt that she ought not to call his name to find out for certain. So somehow she had to make herself go back into the drawing-room and, by herself, face the thing that was concealed behind the big green and white striped couch.

At first it seemed impossible to make herself take a step in that direction. It felt even worse now than it had earlier in the day. She wanted to turn and run from the house, to leave it for ever and leave San Antioco for ever. But really it was only for a few seconds after she had heard the two policemen drive away that she hesitated in the hall and when she went towards the drawing-room, she walked quickly. There was sense, after all, in getting this part of the business over before her panic could mount too high. She had reached the middle of the room before she fully took in the scene before her.

The green and white couch was not in the corner of the room any more. It was against the wall, under the window. There was no dead body in the room. There was no sign that any dead body had ever been in the room. Everything was just as it had been in the morning before there had been any murder. Nothing was out of place. Nothing looked strange or unusual.

It was such a relief to Ruth that at last tears overcame her completely. She dropped into a chair, buried her face in her arms and gave herself up to sobs.

The sensation of it was wonderful. Shock and terror seemed to drain out of her with the streaming tears. She was crying so unrestrainedly that she did not hear a footstep in the hall.

But she heard when the voice of Marguerite Ranzi remarked thoughtfully from the doorway, "So you care all that much, do you ? Lester only laughed about it, of course, but I often wondered. . . ."

VI

RUTH SAT UP with a jerk. She groped for her handkerchief, mopped her face and looked up. As her vision cleared, the first thing she saw was not Marguerite but a detail in the room that she had overlooked when she had reflected that everything there looked just the same as it had before the murder.

Not quite everything looked the same. The silver vase, that had had pink geraniums in it, was now filled with sprays of oleander.

"Mind if I turn the light on?" Marguerite asked and snapped it on before Ruth could answer. "My dear, I don't know what to say, it's so awful. Stephen rang me up and told me and I came as quickly as I could."

"*Stephen* rang you up?" Ruth said incredulously.

"Yes, he was here when they came and told you about it, wasn't he?"

Marguerite walked over to the couch and sat down. She looked distraught and shaken and her face was paler than usual, yet even then she looked, as she always did, a strikingly beautiful woman. She was tall, poised, well-groomed, sleekly blonde, with a fine, pale golden tan and big, placid, blue eyes. This evening she was wearing a white, full-skirted dress that left her shoulders bare, and high-heeled, golden sandals. She always had an air of taking life easily and good-humouredly and though this was somewhat disturbed now, Ruth's show of emotion seemed to surprise and interest her.

"How can I help?" she asked. "There must be all sorts of things that'll have to be done. How does death work in Italy, I wonder. I mean the formalities and so on. I've no experience."

"I haven't got round to thinking about that yet," Ruth said.

"Well, let me know when there's something I can do. You look knocked all of a heap. Poor Lester—I can't take it in yet. But you—you've actually seen him, haven't you?"

"Yes," Ruth said, "I've seen him."

" D'you know, I've never seen a dead person ? "
Marguerite said. " Isn't that extraordinary at my age ? But
listen, my dear, you can't stay here by yourself. You'd
better come and stay with Amedeo and me. You and Nicky,
of course. By the way, where is Nicky ? "

" He hasn't come home yet."

" Is he usually as late as this ? "

" Not usually. Sometimes."

" I wonder where he's got to."

" Yes," Ruth said, " I wonder." She shivered as she
said it, wildly wondering too where a dead body and a bunch
of blood-stained pink geraniums had got to.

Marguerite, sharp-eyed in spite of her casual manner,
observed the shiver, misunderstood it and said, " Yes, it'll
be awful breaking it to him, won't it ? But you know, he
may take it quite well. Quite likely he won't really mind
much. Perhaps not as much as you."

" What d'you mean ? " Ruth asked.

Marguerite did not answer directly, but settling her full
skirt more elegantly, remarked, " Anyway, the two of you
had better move in with us for the time being. Let's go
upstairs now and pack a few things so that you can come
away as soon as he does turn up."

" But I can't," Ruth said. " Thanks, Marguerite, it's
very good of you, but I've got to stay. There are the
Gargiulos to be told and—well, I don't know when Nicky's
going to turn up, so there's nothing for me to do but hang
around."

Marguerite looked at her as if there was something in
Ruth's attitude that puzzled her.

" Well, if you don't want to come, of course . . . By
the way, what happened this afternoon ? Why didn't you
come to see me ? "

" But I did."

" You did ? When ? "

" When you told me to come—about three."

" Did I say three ? Did I really ? So, of course, you must
have been quite annoyed when you didn't find me. You
didn't wait long, I hope. Oh, Lord, I'm sorry."

" I waited quite a while." But Ruth's mind was not on
the question. Marguerite's casualness, that had been so

irritating a few hours earlier, now was unimportant. What Ruth was thinking concerning Marguerite was that she did not show the signs of grief that might have been expected. Marguerite had always claimed to be fond of Lester Ballard. She had often said that she found him very attractive. She had been amused, not repelled by his faults. But now, judging by the look on her face and her manner, Ruth would have said that although Marguerite was distressed by Lester's death, she was not seriously grief-stricken. What was more, she was like someone who has something on her mind, a problem, an uncertainty, and who hopes that this fact about her will pass unnoticed while she tries to think it over.

But Ruth did not think long about this, either. She was grateful for Marguerite's presence, which drove the eeriness out of the house, and she wished that she had been able to accept the invitation to leave the place for the night. But this could not be done. Besides Nicky and Gargiulos, there was Stephen. Sooner or later, she supposed, he would return to tell her how he had managed to get rid of the dead body and to explain to her, in his wisdom, what on earth she was to do next.

Also, Ruth felt, there was an extreme necessity for her to be by herself for a while, so that she could start to think out how it had happened that one man had been found dead in two places at the same time. Not that she had been deceived for a moment that the man in the morgue could be Lester Ballard. Yet, if she had not known that Lester was lying dead in his own home, she might have been deceived. There was a good deal of similarity between the two dead men. Both were small, slight and fair-haired. The chief difference that she had noticed during her one sickened glimpse of the man under the sheet, had been in their hands. The hands of the man in the morgue had been squarer than Lester's, with shorter, thicker fingers and rougher skin, hands that had done hard work, which Lester's never had.

Marguerite at that moment was studying one of her own hands. She was holding it up before her, unthinkingly turning it this way and that, unconsciously admiring it. The puzzled frown had remained on her face.

" The thing I can't make out," she said suddenly, " is what Lester was doing up there this afternoon. Can you ? "

"It was his usual walk," Ruth said, hoping that Marguerite would not insist on discussing it.

"But in the afternoon, on a day as hot as this?" Marguerite peered harder at her hand. "And you told me he'd gone off to Naples for the day," she remarked.

"So far as I knew, he had," Ruth said.

"Yet he came back."

"He must have."

"Didn't you see him?"

"No, I was out most of the day."

"Were you? What were you doing?"

Ruth moved impatiently, thinking that Marguerite was being a little too absent-minded.

"I went for a swim in the morning, then I had lunch with Stephen in San Antioco, then I went to your house, waited quite a time and then came home."

"So you don't know why he came back or anything?"

Something in Marguerite's tone made Ruth look at her more closely.

"Marguerite, do you know something about it?"

"No, but he must have had a reason, mustn't he?" Marguerite said. "I'll tell you what I'm wondering. I'm wondering if he ever went to Naples at all."

"The Gargiulos will know that. They went with him."

"Yes, that's an idea. Only even if they do know . . ." She paused for such a long time that Ruth asked, "Well?"

"Nothing," Marguerite said. "Only I've always had a queer feeling about the Gargiulos. I can't explain it exactly, but I've never trusted them. Not that I'm making any accusation against them."

"Accusation?" Ruth said sharply. "Accusation of what?"

Marguerite's face grew more worried. "No accusation—that's what I said, isn't it? I haven't a single thing against them. But still I never felt that they were quite—right, somehow."

Ruth thought it over. At last she said, "Just what are you really trying to say to me?"

"Well—only that I think it's possible that even if the Gargiulos do know whether or not Lester went to Naples, they might decide not to tell the truth about it."

" Why shouldn't they ? "

" I don't know, I don't know ! " Marguerite said. " I don't know anything about them, it's just a feeling. But there seems to be something queer about the whole thing, doesn't there ? I mean, if it had happened at night, if Lester had come home as usual in the evening and taken his usual evening walk and been run over and killed, then it would just have been a horrible accident and there wouldn't have been anything queer about it. But there *is* something queer about this. You do see that, don't you ? "

Ruth drew a painful breath.

" Yes," she said, " I do see it. But—oh, there's probably an explanation for it all and just now I—I'm sorry, but I simply can't go on talking about it." She put her hands over her face. She felt that she must at any cost shut out the sight of Marguerite, sitting there looking worried, waving her hand backwards and forwards in front of her eyes and uttering her all too reasonable questions.

Marguerite said quickly, " My dear, I'm so sorry. What a fool I am. I was forgetting for the minute what you've been through to-day. Let's talk about something else. Or am I being a nuisance all round ? Would you sooner not talk at all ? "

" No, go on," Ruth said.

But that seemed to silence Marguerite, who now looked at Ruth rather helplessly and plainly could not actually jerk her mind away from the questions that she had been asking. The silence lengthened. They were sitting there like that, each deep in her own thoughts, when the telephone rang.

Ruth picked it up.

Stephen's voice said, " Are you alone ? "

" Marguerite's here," Ruth answered.

" Oh, yes . . . Well, listen and be careful how you answer. I want to see you as soon as possible. Can you get out and meet me ? "

" You could come here," Ruth said.

" No, we've some things to talk over that mustn't be overheard. Has Nicky come in yet ? "

" No."

" Nor the Gargiulos ? "

" No."

" Well, can't you get rid of Marguerite and meet me ? "

" Perhaps. Presently."

" I'll tell you what I'll do. I'll go and wait for you on the cliffs. I'll be sitting around somewhere just beyond the end of those olive groves. I'll wait till you come. All right ? "

" Yes," Ruth said hesitantly. " Yes, quite all right, thank you. And thank you for ringing up."

Hoping that that last reply of hers sounded like thanks for a call made to inquire about the state that she was in, Ruth put down the telephone.

" Stephen," she explained.

Marguerite smiled. " He's nice, isn't he ? He's one of those vague, rather hopeless sort of people who turn out to be awfully warm-hearted and efficient in an emergency. I'm glad he's around. But he told me to-day he isn't staying much longer."

" To-day ? Have you seen him to-day ? " Ruth did not mean to ask the question as sharply as she did.

" Yes, he was down in the cove this afternoon, swimming, when I was . . . Oh, listen, there's someone outside. It may be Amedeo. He said he'd be coming later." Marguerite got up and walked out into the hall.

But it was not her husband whose footsteps she had heard and who now faced her from the doorway. It was Madge and Cesare Gargiulo.

Both showed in their faces a solemn sort of excitement.

" You've heard, then ? " Marguerite said.

Cesare replied, " Yes, *signora*. We heard in San Antioco. Everyone is talking about it. It is a terrible thing."

" Where's Miss Seabright ? " his wife asked abruptly.

" In here."

Marguerite led the way back into the drawing-room.

Madge came quickly after her, with Cesare following more hesitantly. They stood side by side, looking at Ruth with a mixture of sympathy and impatient curiosity, obviously longing to be told all the most distressing details of the tragedy, but having enough sense of propriety to know that first there must be some expressions of grief, horror and commiseration.

Madge Gargiulo had been born in Yorkshire. She was

about thirty-eight, a tall, strongly-built, brisk, capable woman, who in her way was handsome, though there was something harsh and heavy about her features, some fundamental Northern dourness, that made it easy to think of her as plain. Her brown hair was turning grey already and though there was energy, there was not much elasticity about her movements. Her arms and ankles were always scarred by bites of mosquitoes, to which her skin reacted with peculiar intensity. She was short-tempered and often ironic in her speech, and though she seemed always to have liked Ruth and, in an off-hand fashion, to have been ready to do anything she wanted, she had never troubled not to show that she did not like Marguerite Ranzi.

Cesare was very different. He was a dark, quiet man, perhaps a year or two younger than Madge, a slenderly built and graceful person with eager, dark eyes, a brilliant smile and a remarkable and refined art of doing nothing. He did nothing with such subtlety that it was almost a pleasure to watch him. There was no crudity about it, no obvious idleness. He always seemed to be just about to make some important addition to the comfort of the people around him, but except when he was driving the car, which he did with an artist's skill and passion, nothing resulted from it. Lester Ballard had seemed always to delight in the spectacle, saying that Cesare was the cleverest man he had ever met, and that since all the work that Cesare did not do was done very adequately by the untiring Madge, there was no cause for complaint.

When Marguerite started telling Madge that Ruth had been through a dreadful experience that afternoon and needed to be well taken care of, Madge interrupted her brusquely, " Thanks, I know that without being told. I've had enough shocks in my own life to know what's necessary. I haven't always had people fussing round me to save me trouble." She gave Marguerite one of her grim stares, then turned back to Ruth. " Now, love, tell us all about it and get that over, then I'll pack you off to bed and fix up a bit of supper. If only we'd heard about it sooner, we'd have come back right away, but we didn't hear anything till we got to San Antioco. I've been with Cesare's mother all day. The old lady was feeling poorly and didn't want me to leave her. But to think of you being here all by yourself when it happened. I hope those police fellows treated you right. I never have felt I'd really like to trust these foreign policemen. It's not like the ones at home, who'd probably give you a nice strong cup of tea before sending you home again. I'd an uncle was killed in an accident in the mill and the police were right kind. Not that you can always rely on them either and I've known some who were plain brutes and ought to have been behind prison bars themselves. But at any rate, they're not like these foreign ones."

Like a good many Yorkshire people, Madge was often extremely voluble, but always with a taciturn air of scorning to speak an unnecessary word.

While she had been speaking, Marguerite had murmured something about not being needed any more and had slipped away. When she had gone, Madge again asked to be told what had happened that afternoon.

Ruth felt near the end of her endurance. To be alone and have time to think had begun to seem like the only thing that would preserve her sanity and stop her blurting out the real truth to the first person who asked for it. But she knew that she had to do what Madge asked and that it was of the greatest importance to do it convincingly. Madge was observant, had lived in the same house with her for four years and might easily recognise the presence of a fear for which there was no apparent reason.

Speaking jerkily and making the story as short as she could, Ruth told the Gargiulos of the coming of the police, of what they had told her and of how she had had to go with them to identify the dead man as Lester Ballard.

She spoke as if there had never been any doubt on this point. Also she spoke with some incoherence, which came naturally enough, meaning this to suggest that it would be more or less useless to question her too closely just then.

Madge and Cesare seemed to arrive by themselves at this conclusion, for after an exchange of glances, Madge said, " Well, I wouldn't have been in your shoes for anything, love, and I can see you're feeling it badly. So what you're going to do now is go to bed while I get you a bit of supper. I don't suppose you've much appetite, but you'd better have something or you'll feel worse by and by than you do now."

"Thanks, but I'm not going to bed yet," Ruth said. "For one thing, it's much too hot still. I shouldn't rest. But now that you're home to see to things, I think I'll go out for a short walk. I shan't be long."

"Well, maybe some air would do you good," Madge agreed. "I'll be getting some supper for you while you're gone. And for Nicky too, I suppose. But where is he, love? D'you mean he hasn't come home?"

Ruth, who had risen, shook her head wearily.

"No, and I don't know what's happened to him. I think perhaps he heard something in San Antioco, like you did, and got scared or something. You never can tell what he'll do."

"That's right," Madge said, "you never can tell what he'll get up to, except that it won't make much sense."

"If he comes back while I'm gone. . . ." But the problem of what to tell Madge to do if that should happen was beyond Ruth just then. Leaving the sentence unfinished, she went out to look for Stephen.

VII

SHE FOUND him on the cliffs. The glowing tip of his cigarette first showed her where he was. As she came closer, she saw his white shirt and more shadowily, his face. He was not far from the edge of the precipice, stretched out on the grass.

The moon had not yet risen and the evening was very dark. It was filled with all kinds of sweet scents which in the day-time were hardly noticeable.

Ruth sat down on the grass beside Stephen.

"I mustn't stay long," she said.

"Why not?"

"Because of Nicky. He hasn't come back yet and when he does I—I want to be the person who breaks the news to him."

" You worry about him too much," Stephen said. " Other boys have lost their fathers."

" Not quite in this way."

" Well, he isn't going to know about that, is he ? "

She became confused. " No—perhaps not—but even a motor accident, which is what he'll be told, will be an awful shock."

" So you did identify that other man as Ballard ? "

She nodded.

Even in the darkness she could tell that Stephen's eyes were fixed on her face with a peculiar intensity.

After a little pause he asked her, " Was that the best thing to do ? "

Her voice began to shake as she answered, " I don't know ! I'd not time to think. It seemed easiest. If I hadn't done that, there'd have been inquiries straight away and this way we've got a little time. And he did have on Lester's clothes, with all Lester's things in his pockets. And he did look like Lester, more or less. So if they find out that he's someone else, they can't blame me, can they ? They can't prove I didn't honestly believe it was Lester."

" And who was he really ? "

" D'you think I know ? " She was furious with him for asking such a question. " And d'you think I don't realise that sooner or later I'll have to tell the truth about him ? Whoever he is, you can't let a person simply disappear. He may have a wife and children who are already sick from worry about him . . . Oh, I haven't the faintest idea if I did the best thing or not ! Probably I didn't ! Probably it was lunacy, but I felt nearly off my head and it seemed easiest, a sort of godsend to give us time."

Stephen's hand closed over one of hers.

" I expect it was the best thing to do," he said. " Really, the only thing. But we'll have to try on our own to find out who he was."

" But what's happened to Lester himself ? Where did you take him ? How did you manage to move him ? "

The tip of Stephen's cigarette glowed more brightly as he drew at it.

" You were wrong about the car not being there," he said. " It was there, in the garage. And the garage wasn't

locked. When you'd gone, I explored a bit and I found
that one can get from the house to the back-entrance of
the garage without being seen from the road. So I simply
carried Ballard out there and dumped him in the car."

" D'you mean he's there now ? "

" Keep your voice down ! " Stephen said fiercely. " What
d'you take me for ? Of course he isn't there."

" Then what did you do with him ? "   •

" I dumped him in the car, went back to the house and
cleaned up—thank the Lord for that tiled floor !—then I
drove off with him."

" But wasn't it still daylight ? Anyone might have seen
you."

" It was more or less dusk. And it had to be risked, hadn't
it ? "

" Where did you take him ? "

" Up the mountain road."

She peered into his shadowy face in amazement. " You
must be mad, absolutely mad," she said. " There might
have been police there still. Didn't you hear them say that
that was where they found Lester's body ? "

" But there was nowhere else to go. If I'd stuck to the
main road I'd have been bound to pass someone who'd
have recognised the car and known that it was being driven
by the wrong person. Anyway I was lucky. They'd
gone."

" But where did you put him ? Where is he now ? "

There was another pause.

" I haven't made up my mind yet whether or not I'm
going to tell you."

His tone was quiet but there was something in it that
made Ruth's heart start thumping.

" And why not ? " she asked.

" Well, in case you should suddenly decide to start talking
to the police. From your face, there was a moment this
afternoon when I thought you were going to. And I don't
want that to happen without my knowing about it. I've
put myself in your hands, haven't I ? And without knowing
what's been going on."

" I'm in your hands, too," she said. Yet it was only as
she said this that she fully realised its truth. Until then

she had been thinking of Stephen as an ally, as someone who surprisingly and in a way disturbingly, had come to her aid. Now she was suddenly not certain if he had come to her aid at all. "Anyway, why did you do what you've done?" she asked. "Nobody made you do it, or even asked you to do it. You came in and found me there with Lester and you could have rung up the police straight away."

"Which is something I've been telling myself at frequent intervals ever since I didn't do it," Stephen said.

"Well, you can do it still, if you want to."

"No, I can't."

"Nobody's stopping you," she said, her anger rising.

"Don't be a damn fool," he answered. "I'm in it now as much as you are. Only I still don't know what's been going on. So if you don't know what's happened to Lester, it brings in a touch of equality."

"I think I know where he is," she said. "There are those ruined huts at the end of the ravine. He's there, isn't he?"

"Possibly. Now go on and tell me what's really happened, then we'll try to work out the next step together."

"You still haven't told me why you didn't call the police."

"Well, I didn't and that's that."

"You'd no reason?"

"If you like, I'd no reason."

"Yet you thought it was I who'd killed Lester. You still do. When I told you that I'd walked in only just ahead of you and found him like that, you didn't believe me. And now you think that by scaring me, you can make me tell you some other story. But that is what happened and I'm not going to tell you any other story." Her anger had mounted so much that, while she was speaking, she almost believed that what she had told him had been the whole truth and that he had no possible right to want to know more.

The way she spoke had some effect on him, for after another slight hesitation, he replied, "I'm not trying to scare you. I really didn't mean to do that. And though I did think, when I walked in, that you'd killed him. . . . Good God, if you'd seen your face! But that could have been fright, I suppose. . . . Well, that business of the

clothes and then those police walking in with another dead
Ballard on their hands, made it pretty clear that there's
much more in the whole affair than I thought during those
first few minutes. But I still want to know what you know
about it."

"No more than you do, Stephen. Really, I don't. And
I feel as if I might go mad if I don't get a chance soon to
think it all over and try to make some sense of it."

"I've made a little sense of it—I think," Stephen said,
"and if it weren't for that phoney alibi of yours, I'd be
quite ready to believe that you don't fit in. But that still
needs some explaining."

Ruth was taken completely by surprise. "Phoney alibi?
What alibi? What d'you mean?"

"That visit to Marguerite. I knew there was something
odd about it at the time, but I thought it was just a dodge
for getting rid of me, so I didn't say anything."

Ruth shook her head helplessly. "I don't understand
at all. There was nothing queer about it. Marguerite had
invited me some days before, then she rang me up this
morning to remind me about it and told me to come early.
So that was why I went there straight after lunch. I wasn't
trying to get rid of you. Why should you think I'd want to
do that, anyway?"

"All the same, you never went to her house, did you?"

"I certainly did. And waited for about an hour, even
though she wasn't there."

"Can you prove it—I mean, that you went there, or
even that she asked you?"

"Perhaps not that I went there. I'm not sure about that.
I'm not sure if anyone saw me. But you've only to ask
Marguerite herself to find out if she expected me or not."

He gave her another of his disturbing glances. "You
see, Marguerite rang me up this morning and asked me
to meet her on the rocks down here after lunch. And
that appointment she remembered, because I found her
here."

Ruth's throat went tight. "Then it's Marguerite who'll
have to do some explaining. All the same . . ."

"Well?"

"If you'd an appointment here with Marguerite, why did

you ask me to go to Ravento with you? Or don't you remember doing that?"

"Of course I remember."

"Why did you do it, then?"

"Because you seemed so damned depressed that I thought I'd try to do something to cheer you up. But the idea didn't attract you, so I dropped it."

"But if you'd an appointment with Marguerite . . ."

"I hadn't promised anything."

Ruth heard herself give an uneasy laugh. "Well, I don't understand all this bit of it, but we can clear it up by talking to Marguerite." She did not believe that Stephen would have missed a chance of seeing Marguerite for the sake of trying to cheer up anyone else, but she did not want to go on probing into that too far, when a few questions to Marguerite would solve the problem. "Now I mustn't stay much longer, Stephen. I said to the Gargiulos that I'd just come out for some air and I don't want them to start wondering where I've got to. So tell me quickly what you mean when you said you could make some sense of all this."

"I don't think I could tell you quickly," he said. "I'll have to think it out a bit more first. But there's one thing I meant to tell you. You know those clothes that Ballard was wearing?"

"Yes."

"Well, I've got them. I haven't had time to examine them carefully to see if they'll tell us anything, but I thought they might be important, so—well, as soon as you went off with those policemen, I undressed him and I took a rug from a cupboard upstairs and rolled him up in that. I'll go through the pockets and so on carefully this evening and let you know what I find."

"I see." She got to her feet. But she did not go away at once. She stood there, staring across the bay at the lights of Naples, sparkling in a bright band along the horizon. "I want to try and say something, but I don't quite know how." She paused again. "It's just that . . . Stephen, you and I don't really know each other, do we? I mean, we don't know much about each other, where we come from or anything like that. And yet now suddenly we're tied up

in this thing together, and you seem to be trying to help me
and I'm grateful—truly I'm grateful—only I can't make out
what's happened and——"

" It's all right," he said. " Don't go on. I'll see you
sometime to-morrow and tell you if there's anything of
interest about those clothes."

" All right. Good night, Stephen."

" Good night."

She turned and set off. But after a couple of steps, she
paused. " He is in those ruined huts, isn't he ? "

" Yes."

She went on up the steep, paved path between the olive
groves.

As soon as she reached the terrace, Madge Gargiulo,
who must have been listening for her footsteps, came to the
door to meet her. Ruth saw at once that Madge had been
crying, for her eyelids were red and swollen, but her manner
was as brisk as usual.

" There's no sign of that boy Nicky," she said, " but
Signor Ranzi's here. He's in the drawing-room. I told him
you'd only gone out for a short walk and he said he'd wait.
Shall I tell him that you don't want to see him ? If you
like, I'll tell him you're too tired to see anyone."

" No, I'd better see him," Ruth said, though the thought
of seeing yet another person was almost unbearable.

Amedeo Ranzi was sitting on the green and white striped
couch under the window. He rose as she appeared. He was a
tall man, though with a stoop that made him seem less tall
than he was. He was about fifty and his age was marked on
his face by unusually deep lines. There was generally a look
of weariness about him, too, an appearance of trying to spare
himself effort. His black hair and moustache had become
iron-grey and his skin was sallow. His manner was always
rather stiff. He looked like a man whose health has never
been good and who has concentrated on dignity to make up
for a lack of vitality. He was wearing a spotless suit of
white linen, perfectly pressed.

Taking Ruth's hand with a firm pressure, he said, " I
know it all. You have no need to talk or to tell me anything.
I came only to say that whatever I can do, you must com-
mand it. I am sorry I could not come sooner but I have

been in Naples all day and have only just returned. As soon as I had heard your dreadful news from Marguerite, I came. I will not try to tell you my feelings. Lester has been my good friend for years and his death is a great shock to me. But it is of all of you here that I have been thinking. His poor boy . . . How is he ? "

" I don't know. He isn't here," Ruth said.

Ranzi's eyebrows lifted sharply. " He has gone away ? "

" I don't know. He hasn't been home since the morning. He went off to Professor Bruno as usual after breakfast and he hasn't been back. I'm worried about it, of course. I think he must have heard something in San Antioco about his father's death and for some reason can't face coming home." The lies came with increasing ease.

" And you have done nothing yet to trace him ? " There was astonished reproof in the words.

Ruth said defensively, " I didn't know what to do. I thought it was probably best to wait till he came home of his own accord."

" But it's so late. Surely you at least rang up Professor Bruno to find out when he left there."

" No."

Ranzi looked at her keenly. " Forgive me," he said next. " You have been through an ordeal. You could not think of everything. How I wish that I could have come sooner. Marguerite told me she came but that you would not let her do anything for you. But now at least I can take this matter of the boy off your hands. I will ring up Professor Bruno and if he can tell me nothing of where Nicky went when he left him, I will telephone to the police and let them know that he's missing."

" No ! " This was what Ruth had known would come sooner or later. Sooner or later she would not be able to prevent it. But at least she could make an effort to delay the beginning of the hunt. " No, Amedeo, please don't do that, not the police, not yet. Ring Professor Bruno by all means—of course I ought to have done that myself—but let's not ring the police before to-morrow morning. If Nicky hasn't come back by then, we'll have to ask them to help us find him, but I'd far sooner give him time to come back of his own accord, which I think he will quite soon now, than have a sort of hue and cry out after him, probably terrifying him out of his wits."

Ranzi looked uncertain. "Madge told me that Nicky and Lester had a quarrel this morning. Is that the trouble, d'you think? A boy like that might blame himself, feeling that his angry thoughts against his father must have had some part in his death."

"Oh, it wasn't really so much of a quarrel." Ruth had forgotten until then that there had been any witness to that scene but herself. Wondering if there was any chance of stopping Madge repeating the story to other people, without arousing Madge's own suspicions, she added, "But you may be right. Nicky didn't exactly love his father and it may be the thought of that that's upsetting him now and making him try to keep away from everybody. Anyway, I'd give him a little more time to argue it out by himself."

Ranzi nodded. "Yes, after all, I think you are right. You understand the boy so well. How fortunate it is for him now that you are here. He loves you so much, he knows you care for him. I'm fond of Nicky, you know. I've always thought he had fine qualities and a good intelligence and that all he needed to start developing fully was a little patience and affection. But so few people have patience. Lester had no patience—none. And he was a greedy man. He could never be satisfied with what he had. He had to have more and then more and more still. So he had no time to give his child, no interest, no tenderness. I do not blame Nicky if he had guilty wishes in him that his father should die. I do not blame him at all. . . . Now I will ring up Professor Bruno." He said the last few words hurriedly, as if he regretted having spoken as he had, and went to the telephone.

Ruth looked at him with a new concentration. So Amedeo Ranzi after all was not so very fond of his good friend Lester Ballard. But Ruth did not want him to think that she had taken any special notice of his words. While he was telephoning she went to a window, pushed the shutters open on to the warm night and leant her elbows on the window-sill. The moon was rising now and lighting up the dark masses of the mountains.

The conversation on the telephone became excited. Then

in a number of polite expressions, it died down. Ranzi turned towards her.

" Nicky has not been there all day," he said.

" What, not this morning ? " Ruth asked.

" No, not all day. But apparently this is not altogether unusual. He absents himself quite often and in my opinion the professor has said nothing about it because he has no objection to being paid for work he has not been called upon to do. However that may be, to-day Nicky has not been to see him at all. In fact, he has been missing since the morning. Are you still sure that we ought not to ask the police to-night to help us find him ? "

Ruth leant her forehead on her hands. Her head felt hot, while her hands seemed unnaturally cool.

" Let's wait till the morning," she said.

She felt Ranzi's look upon her and tried not to shrink from it.

It seemed a long time before he said, " Very well, if you are sure."

" Yes, I'm sure he'll be back before then," she answered, trying hard to make it sound as if she believed it.

Soon after that Ranzi went home.

Ruth went out on to the terrace with him. Until that evening she had always felt intimidated by him. There was something in his manner, a pride, a jealousy of his position, which, it had seemed to her, put a barrier round him through which only a favoured few, of which she had never been one, were expected to pass. Yet to-night she had not felt this. His kindness had seemed simple and real, and she was sincerely grateful for it.

All the same, she was relieved that his visit was over. Now she had only Madge to face, then she could go to bed.

Madge turned out to be easy to handle. She had become really taciturn, in fact, almost surly. Bringing Ruth some supper on a tray, she put it down and went out of the room without a word. Ruth guessed that she was trying to keep tears at bay. Starting on the omelet that Madge had made, Ruth thought how strangely people could surprise one. A few hours ago who could have guessed that out of all the people who had known Lester Ballard, the only one to weep at his death would be Madge Gargiulo ?

The omelet and the coffee were soon finished and Ruth went up to her bedroom.

This was the time that she had appointed with herself for some clear thinking. This was the time, quietly walking up and down her room, when she had intended to make up her mind on some of the questions that at present only churned her thoughts into confusion. There was the question of what had made her so determined at all costs to shield Nicky, to give him time, to give him some faint chance of escape, and there was the question of whether or not this feeling of hers had led her into anything but a wanton and ugly error, a betrayal of justice, which she and perhaps others would come bitterly to regret. Yet now the answers to these questions did not seem very important. Of course she had simply acted out of her love for Nicky, before she had had time to consider the meaning of his guilt, and, of course, given the same circumstances, she would act in the same way again and again think afterwards. The real point of confusion in her mind now was the connection between the deaths of the two Lester Ballards and how Nicky had come to be involved in them. That he could kill in a sudden rage she had found easy enough to imagine, but that he could co-operate cold-bloodedly in a murder plot was hardly to be thought of.

The probability seemed to be that Nicky had blundered, with his own rage and hatred, into the middle of a murder plot hatched by someone else, and had added a death to it that had not been intended.

Ruth started to think about Stephen. As she did so, her eyes lighted on something on her dressing-table. It was a box of matches.

But why should a box of matches suddenly hold her attention, as if there were something of special importance about it ?

Then she recollected that this was the box that had been lying on the table on the terrace when she had returned in the afternoon from her unsuccessful visit to Marguerite. Stephen was always losing his matches and later that afternoon, when he had walked in and found her stooping

over the body of Lester Ballard, he had had no matches.
She had had to fetch some from the kitchen. Did that
mean anything ?

In the morning, she remembered, Stephen had sat on the
terrace while she had been upstairs changing her dress.
The matches might have been left behind on the table then.
In that case, they were not of any importance. But suppose
they had been left on the table later, during the time that
she had been at the Ranzis'.

Leaning against the dressing-table, half closing her eyes,
she tried to remember whether or not Stephen had had any
matches in the restaurant when he and she had had lunch.
Who had lit the cigarettes they had smoked then, he or she ?

There was no doubt about it, Stephen had done so.

Her hand, which had been on the match-box, jerked away
from it as if it had just burst into flame. But at that moment
something else in the room caught her attention. Neither
the red and white handkerchief that she had worn on her
head when she had gone down to bathe, nor her sun-glasses,
were where she had left them.

She knew that she had left them on the dressing-table.
She was certain of that, for she always left them there.
Always, when she had taken them off, she immediately
combed out her hair, facing the mirror. It was one of those
habitual actions about which she could not be mistaken.
But now the handkerchief was hanging on a peg on the wall
and the sun-glasses were on the table beside the bed.

She had started shivering. She could not stop it, though
she was only half-aware of why that small alteration in her
room should give her such a sense of shock. But after only
a moment she began moving rapidly about, opening drawers,
looking in cupboards, and as she did so the thing that she
had guessed at became plain. Very little was disarranged,
only a jacket on a wrong hanger, a pair of shoes in the
wrong place, the blue cotton dress that she had worn that
morning over her bathing suit, on a chair instead of on the
bed where she had thrown it. Yet the thing was proved to her
beyond argument.

" But why ? " she asked herself in a desperate whisper.
" Why, in heaven's name ? What were they looking for ? "

VIII

SHE SCARCELY slept that night. Now and then she dozed, but each time she woke with a feeling of relief at waking, her sleep had been so haunted. During the darkness a feeling of aloneness grew in her, such as she had not known since the first weeks after her mother's death. That had been the end of all family life for her, the putting away of her childhood and the past. Sometimes, during her mother's hopeless illness, which Ruth had been released from the army to tend, the day that finished the struggle had seemed to promise release. Yet in fact what that day had brought had been the feeling that in a terrifying and dangerous world there was now no one to turn to, no one to listen to, no one to trust. To escape from this, she had answered an advertisement. She had been interviewed and been accepted. She had come to San Antioco. Now in the darkness the old, utterly forlorn feeling had returned to her.

Though she did not really expect Nicky to return, she listened continually. The daylight came without the sound of footsteps in the house or of doors opening and closing. There was no movement at all until, at about seven o'clock, Madge went briskly down the stairs. Then shutters were thrown back and the terrace was vigorously swept.

Soon after hearing this, Ruth got up and had a cold shower. The night had been stifling and she felt clammily hot and exhausted.

It was a little cooler on the terrace than in the house. There was a faint breeze this morning and even a few little puffs of white cloud in the sky. The breeze had blown away the haze in the air and the mountains across the bay stood out as barren masses of rock, appearing both nearer and higher than they had yesterday, when the mist had softened their starkness. The sea had turned a more brilliant blue, with its surface broken into ripples that dazzlingly reflected the light.

Coffee made Ruth feel a little better. Madge, who brought it to her, had no tears in her eyes this morning, but it was

plain that she also had not slept much. Tiredness and
worry had the effect on her of sending her about her work
with an air of sullen determination. She looked as if
she resented having to do the work, but as if she would
resent even more any suggestion that she should leave it
undone.

Dumping the tray down in front of Ruth, she said,
"That Nicky hasn't come home, I suppose you know.
What a lad he is, not worrying two pins how much he upsets
other people. Well, one thing good that'll come out of all
this, I said to Cesare, is we won't have to put up with him
and his tantrums any more. The next job we get, there
aren't going to be any temperaments around like him and
his father. I've had enough of that sort to last me the rest
of my time, thank you very much."

"Yet you were rather fond of Mr. Ballard, weren't you,
Madge?" Ruth said.

"Fond?" Madge said. "What d'you mean by that, may
I ask?"

"Well, last night you were crying."

"Oh, that." A sardonic look showed on Madge's face.
She stooped to scratch a mosquito bite on her ankle. "That
wasn't for him—though he was all right, of course. I'd
never have stayed on if I hadn't liked him well enough. He
didn't interfere and he didn't count the pennies, as if one
wasn't to be trusted. He was a gentleman all right and I
didn't mind working for him. I could never stay with anyone
who stood over me, pretending to know my work better than
I do myself. Well, there was nothing of that about Mr.
Ballard, and I've been happy enough here, and I suppose
I'm sorry to be going away, but I wasn't crying about all
that."

"What had upset you then?"

Madge shrugged. "Well, death makes you think, doesn't
it? We've most of us had deaths to cry about, one time or
another, and one thing sometimes reminds you of another.
It was just foolishness, all the same. And being scared,
maybe."

"Scared?" Ruth swallowed some coffee so suddenly that
it stung her throat. "What's there to scare you?"

Madge shrugged again. "Oh, I'm a fool, I know that. But I'm always scared of things I can't understand."

"What is it that you don't understand?"

Madge looked at her queerly. Ruth thought for an instant that she did not intend to answer, then Madge said, "Quite a few things, love." A look of amusement, a compressing of the lips that was like resistance to a smile, appeared on her tired, dourly handsome face. It was almost as if she were daring Ruth to question her further.

Perhaps Ruth would have done so. She was deeply startled by Madge's tone. But at that moment Ruth became aware that a car, that had been coming noisily up the hill from San Antioco, had stopped at the gate. It was a police jeep. Several men got out of it. One of them was a man in an ordinary suit of grey gaberdine with a felt hat on his head. Another was the big, bald-headed *Commissario* whom Ruth had seen the day before. Another was the dark-haired *maresciallo*. They came up the steps on to the terrace and approached Ruth, who had risen. The *Commissario* came first and wished her good-morning, then he introduced the man in the grey suit as Signor Cirio, an *agente* from the *Questura*.

Ruth rapidly translated these words to herself. An *agente* from the *Questura*—a detective. So something had gone wrong already. Detectives were not sent out from the *Questura* to inquire into ordinary motor accidents. Something was already suspected. Taking a long look into the face of the man in plain clothes, she thought that perhaps this was the first occasion in her life when she had been knowingly face to face with an enemy.

He was a man probably in his late thirties. He was of medium height and rather thin, with a thin face, narrow and long and pallid. The dark moustache on his lip was no thicker than his sharply-curved, dark eyebrows. His hair was straight and dark. His chin was blueish and had a deep cleft in it. There was an air of indifference about him, almost of boredom. After the introduction to Ruth, he scarcely glanced at her, but stood looking with a detached stare at the bright sparkle of the sea in the bay. In what followed he took hardly any part, yet Ruth had the feeling that the scene was his scene, that he was silently controlling it and that all that happened was according to his plan.

It began with the *Commissario* telling Ruth that they would prefer to speak to her alone, at which, without a word, Madge turned and walked away. As this happened, Ruth saw out of the corner of her eye a face at an upper window. It was Cesare, listening and intent. He vanished again immediately, but Ruth for a moment wondered whether or not she ought to tell the policemen that any conversation held on the terrace was likely to be overheard. But she suspected that the *agente* from the *Questura* had also seen the face at the window and had chosen not to remark on it.

The *Commissario* went on, " I'm sorry to say, *signorina*, we come this morning with some very serious news. Since speaking to you yesterday, we have made a discovery concerning the death of Signor Ballard which puts a completely different complexion on the supposed accident on the mountain road."

" Supposed accident, Signor Commissario ? " Ruth saw her own hand tighten on the edge of the table, the knuckles whitening.

" It was no accident, *signorina*. It was murder."

She had known it was coming. She had known that in that sentence she would hear the word murder spoken. Yet she could only stare at him.

He seemed to find nothing out of order in her silence.

" I am sorry to bring such news," he said. " But no other conclusion is possible."

" But how ? Why ? " She only just managed to bring out the words.

" I can tell you how. I can tell you roughly when. But why, and that other question you have not asked, by whom, we shall not be able to answer for you until after we have taken our inquiries farther than at present."

Ruth drew her breath in slowly. " D'you mean he was knocked down deliberately by that car that ran over him ? "

" No," the big man said. " He was dead already when the car ran over him. He was killed by a shot through the head. Probably this happened about three o'clock. A bit sooner, a bit later, one cannot be sure. But it happened at least half an hour before his body was put in the road and run over, perhaps several times, by a heavy car, then taken up and thrown over the precipice, where, if it had not been caught in the trees, it would probably still be lying undiscovered."

Again Ruth found it easiest to be silent. She felt very little shock at this new information, indeed it was almost as if she had been waiting for something of the sort.

But now the *Commissario* was silent. The group of men on the terrace seemed to be waiting for her to make the next move.

At last she said, " Did you know this yesterday when you sent for me ? "

The *Commissario* made a little shrugging gesture, which could have meant yes or no.

At that point Cirio, the man from the *Questura*, put in a question. " Signor Ballard had a son, hadn't he ? "

" Yes," Ruth said.

" Is he here ? "

" No." But she saw that the abruptness of her answer roused their attention so she made herself go on. " He's been missing since yesterday morning. Nobody knows what's happened to him. I was going to telephone this morning, asking you to help us find him. What we think is that he must have heard the news of his father's death and for some reason felt that he couldn't face coming home. He's a very emotional, unstable boy who never acts as one expects him to."

" Was he much attached to his father ? "

She did her best to imitate the non-committal shrug of the *Commissario*.

It was the *Commissario* who went on. " But weren't you anxious already yesterday over his disappearance ? "

" Oh, yes, but I still hoped he'd come home during the night, and when I discussed it with Signor Ranzi yesterday evening, we decided that we'd wait till this morning before setting a search going. Now I feel we were wrong, but at the time I never dreamt that Nicky would stay out all night."

" He has never done such a thing before ? "

" Oh no."

" How old is he ? "

" Sixteen—and very young for his age."

The man from the *Questura* asked another question, " Can he drive a car ? "

" No," Ruth said.

" Not at all ? You're quite sure ? "

" Quite sure. And what's more "—she turned her head to look the man full in the face—" I should be most surprised if he has any knowledge whatever of firearms."

He met her gaze for a moment, then looked away again at the bay. Ruth found with surprise that it was difficult to think of him as an enemy. He was too detached, too fundamentally uninterested in the human side of the situation to be anyone's enemy.

" Now, now, *signorina*," the *Commissario* said smoothly, " no one is leaping to conclusions. We merely ask questions. There are a great many questions we must ask. We must ask you questions about yourself, too. But it is strange, this affair of the boy disappearing like this, so naturally we ask about him first. Now tell us, did the boy take any part yet in his father's business ? "

" None at all," Ruth said.

" He took no interest in it, knew nothing about it ? "

" No."

" And you ? Did Signor Ballard tell you much about his business ? "

" Very little. Sometimes if he'd picked up some bargain he was particularly pleased about, or if he'd sold something at a very good price to a rich American, he'd talk about it to us, the way people do when something's gone well, but that was all."

" And these bargains he told you about, what were they usually ? Furniture ? Pictures ? Jewels ? "

" I don't think he dealt in jewels at all," she said, " except just a few oddments to catch the eye of the tourist. Pictures and furniture were what he dealt in."

" So he didn't deal in jewels ? "

" Not that I know of."

" Are you acquainted with his manager, Signor Sebastiano ? "

" I've met him a few times. May I ask a question now ? "

" Please."

" Was this murder connected with Signor Ballard's business ? "

He threw up his hands. " But it is much too soon to ask that question. And if, as you say, he did no business in jewels, in valuable jewels, which he might have had in his pocket, then it looks as if we were right yesterday that he had not been robbed. For, you understand, even a gold cigarette-case might have been left behind if something of far greater value had been taken. But you say he did no business in jewels."

She noticed the way that he reiterated the word, as if he thought that sooner or later she would react to it. She thought for a moment, then said, " I'm only saying that I never heard him speak of it. You believe, though, that he did. You do, don't you ? "

" Oh, as to what one believes . . ." Another shrug dismissed it. " Now think carefully, *signorina*. This is an important question. Have you at any time seen any suspicious characters about here, anyone whose presence troubled you for some reason, even if you could not say why ? Have you ever seen Signor Ballard in the company of any such person ? "

She was beginning to shake her head when a thought struck her and she checked the movement almost before she had started it.

The *Commissario* said, " Ah, you have."

" I don't know," she said. " It might have been nothing."

" Tell us, however."

" It was yesterday morning. A man sitting on the wall out there. He just sat and watched the house. At first I didn't think much about it. I thought he was just having a rest there. That was after breakfast. But when I came back from a bathe at least two hours later, he was still there."

" Describe him if you can."

" He was smallish and rather slight and fair-haired, and he had on a checked shirt with a sprig of bougainvillea in his buttonhole. That's all I noticed, really, except that . . ."

" Yes ? "

" Well, I can't explain what made me think it, but somehow I got the idea that he wasn't Italian."

" His fair hair, perhaps."

"Perhaps, though as a matter of fact . . . No, I know what it was, but it sounds stupid."

"Go on."

"He had a hand in a pocket and he was jingling some coins. That was it."

"Aha, I understand. In Italy one can often go for weeks with no coins, with nothing but little crumpled notes, in one's pockets. Is that what you mean?"

"Yes."

"Yet occasionally one has coins. Or he might have been jingling some keys in his pockets."

"I know. There was nothing to go on really. I said it sounded stupid."

"Yet you have this feeling that he was a foreigner. Did he speak to you, perhaps?"

"No. I thought he was going to, but he seemed to change his mind."

"Well, perhaps this is useful information. We shall make inquiries to find out if anyone else saw this stranger in a checked shirt. And now we must ask you some questions about yourself. They are routine questions which we must also put to the other members of the household. When we have done that we shall go over the house. Now to begin with, how long have you worked for Signor Ballard?"

Ruth told him, and, as he put more questions, went on to give him an account of what she had done the day before. There was a great deal that she had to be careful to leave out, but there seemed to be no traps in his questions and the inquiry went quickly. Yet when finally the *Commissario* said that that was all for the present, she felt as if she had been answering his questions for hours.

She offered to fetch the Gargiulos for him, if he wanted to speak to them next. He replied that he would not trouble her and could find them for himself. As he said this, he started towards the house. The little incident disturbed Ruth. It meant that he did not want her to have any chance of talking to either Gargiulo until after he had questioned them. Following the men into the house, she saw them look around in the hall and then move uncertainly into the drawing-room.

She did not go in after them. Standing waiting in the

hall, she was thankful that there was no means by which the pounding of the heart could be discerned by the naked eye. It felt horrible to know that they were probably looking at the very spot where Lester Ballard had died. It was as if the stains that Stephen had washed from the tiled floor must inevitably develop there under their gaze, like invisible writing emerging in the heat of a flame. However, they stayed in the room for only a minute or two, then went off to the kitchen, in search of Madge.

Only the young *maresciallo* who had come to the house the day before, lingered in the room for a moment after the others had gone. From where she stood, Ruth could see him and when she realised why he was lingering, she felt the worst pang of fear that she had known that morning.

It was the arrangement of the room that was puzzling him. Plainly it was not quite as he remembered it, though at first he could not identify the change. Then he looked at the green and white striped couch under the window. Next he looked at the corner of the room.

After that he turned and came out into the hall. As he passed Ruth on his way to the kitchen he smiled at her but did not say anything.

IX

THE POLICE stayed with Madge for longer than they had with Ruth. Afterwards they had an even longer talk with Cesare. Then they spent some time in Lester Ballard's bedroom. They also spent some time in Nicky's room, but to Ruth's relief they did not pay much attention to the drawing-room.

Several times during the morning the telephone rang. Some calls were from acquaintances in San Antioco who had heard of the accident and were ringing up with condolences. One call was from Amedeo Ranzi, anxious to know whether or not Nicky had returned. When Ruth said that Nicky had not come back yet, Ranzi suggested that he should get in touch with the police for her, to ask their help in finding the missing boy. Ruth told him that this was unnecessary, since the police were in the house and already had been told of Nicky's disappearance.

Something stopped her telling Ranzi what had brought the police to the house. From his voice she could tell that he was startled at hearing that they were there, but he did not press her with questions.

Another call was from Stephen.

She had been waiting for this call with growing anxiety. It was of the greatest importance that she should see him soon. But with the police still in the house, she did not want to say so. Fortunately Stephen said it for her, though he began by asking, " Anyone your end who can overhear ? "

" Yes," she said.

" Besides the Gargiulos ? "

" Yes."

" Trouble ? "

So somehow he had guessed, or even had known, that the police were likely to be in the villa just then. Ruth did not like that. She answered, " Yes, serious trouble."

He considered this for a moment, then said, " Well, I've got to see you, and soon. There's something I've got to show you. How shall we work it ? "

" I'll be in all day, I expect," she said. " Nicky hasn't come home yet. I'll have to go on waiting around for him."

" No, that won't do," Stephen said. " You'll have to come here. This thing I want to show you, I can't tote it around."

" What is it ? "

He did not answer that. " How soon can you come ? " he asked. " No—wait a moment. It might not look too good if you dash out and come straight here. Come down to the *piazza* when you can. I'll be having a drink in that café we went to yesterday. I'll wait till you come. But try to make it look casual."

" I see," Ruth said reluctantly. " All right, the *piazza*."

" It's important."

" Yes, I understand. By the way . . ." She did not know what possessed her at that moment, for she had the feeling that she was doing something foolish and dangerous, yet she could not keep back the words. " Do you know that you left a box of matches here yesterday ? "

"Did I? Quite likely. I'm always losing the damn things . . ." He stopped, as if he had only just realised that she had made the remark for a reason. "Well, tell me about that when you see me," he said.

"Yes. Remind me."

She heard him ring off.

Putting the telephone down, she turned and saw that she was being watched from the doorway by the *maresciallo*.

He smiled at her again.

"How do you feel to-day?" he asked. "No more fainting?"

"No," she said.

"Pity," he said. "Yesterday when you fainted it was I who picked you up and put you on the couch."

"That was very kind of you," she said.

"You do not remember?"

"No."

"Pity," he said and turned and went away.

Ruth took a look at the couch, but feeling that if she went on looking at it, she would see its cushions begin to bulge with its horrible secrets, she fled out on to the terrace.

It was nearly noon when the police went away. The party drove away in the jeep and Ruth went looking for Madge and Cesare to find out what they had to say now that the death of their employer had been officially labelled murder. Also she had to tell them that she was going into San Antioco, although this, at the moment, was liable to make them look at her strangely. The best way to do it, she thought, was to tell them that she was going to the Ranzis to give them the new facts about Lester Ballard's death. She went to the kitchen, expecting to find both Gargiulos there. But the room was empty.

It was in the garage that she finally found Cesare. He was cleaning the car, humming a mournful tune while he did so.

Seeing Ruth in the doorway, he straightened up and said, "My poor Madge is sick. Imagine that. Ten years married and never sick until now. But murder is murder." He sounded, however, reasonably cheerful about it.

"What's the matter with her?" Ruth asked.

" Her stomach. Sick. No need to worry."

Ruth wondered if there was anything on earth that would make Cesare worry.

" Where is she ? " she asked.

" Lying down. I gave her a good glass of cognac and sent her to her room. She will soon recover. She is as strong as a horse."

" That's what I always thought," Ruth said.

" And me you thought of as frail, eh, lazy, not much use ? " He smiled good humouredly. " But these strong people, sometimes their nerves are not so strong as they think, and just when they need their strength, it betrays them. You know that feeling yourself, eh ? You think you are strong. But you take care. It is from inside we are always betrayed, just when we least expect it."

Ruth stared at him.

" What have I got to betray ? " she asked.

His face still wore its unconcerned and pleasant smile.

" The heart, the heart," he said. " Like my poor Madge, you think you can conceal the feelings of your heart. I see it all."

" I don't know what on earth you mean," Ruth said, genuinely bewildered by this statement, but less disturbed than she had been at first.

" But I tell no one what I have seen," he said. " For the feelings of the heart I have a great respect. The heat of passion, the loss of reason, all these things I understand. This Signor Ballard, he was a very fascinating man, no ? To an Englishwoman he was irresistible ? I see it all now. It is all quite clear to me."

Ruth studied him with interest.

" Cesare, do you think you're saying something, or are you just having fun ? " she asked.

" Fun ? " he said. " You think I would ever make fun of death, love or religion ? "

" That's how it seems," Ruth said.

" You misunderstand me." Looking offended, he turned to the car again, opened the door nearest to him, leant inside and started polishing the windscreen.

" Well, I came here because I want to tell Madge something," Ruth said, " but since she isn't feeling well, I won't trouble her. Will you give her a message from me when you see her?"

Cesare only polished harder.

"I'm going to see the Ranzis," Ruth went on, "to tell them what the police have told us. Signor Ranzi might be able to advise us what to do; besides, I think he and his wife ought to know what's happened. They were friends of Mr. Ballard's."

"Yes, yes. You have no need to explain to me where you are going."

That checked Ruth in what she had been about to say next. Cesare had never spoken to her like that before.

She hesitated, then said, "I wanted to ask Madge to keep a look out for Nicky."

"She does not need to be told that." He stooped and picked up something from the floor of the car, tossed it out so that it fell near Ruth's feet, then went on polishing the windscreen. The object he had tossed out was a withered geranium.

For a horrible instant, Ruth felt certain that he had done it deliberately. She felt that this gesture had been a declaration of knowledge, a warning, a threat. But his face was as unconcerned as usual, and he did not give a second glance at the flower.

She turned to go. It was possible, she supposed, that he had picked up the geranium merely because he did not hold with withered flowers on the floor of his beloved car, and she did her best to believe this. As she left the garage, she heard Cesare start to hum again the same sweet and mournful tune that he had been humming when she had entered.

Walking down the hill to San Antioco, Ruth started to think over the fact that she had never known before what a natural liar she was. She found herself lying willingly and easily and even feeling rather resentful at having one of her lies detected. But it was evident that she was not quite clever enough. Cesare had guessed that there was something wrong with her explanation of why she wanted to go into San Antioco, so what had she done wrong? Had she said too much, or talked too fast, or had the look on her face given her away? If she was to depend on lies to make her way to safety, that was the sort of thing that she would have to learn.

In the *piazza*, she saw Stephen at once. He was sitting at a table on the pavement outside the café where they had had their drinks the day before. But to Ruth's annoyance, he was not alone. Marguerite Ranzi was with him, wearing a strapless black and white cotton dress with a thick rope of coral round her neck. She had a glass of iced coffee on the table before her and her eyes were intently on Stephen's face. They were talking so earnestly that they did not notice Ruth until she was standing beside their table. On seeing her, neither looked particularly glad at being interrupted. But Stephen at least managed to invite her to join them. He was looking as unkempt as usual and the reddened skin on his forehead had begun to peel.

Sitting down, Ruth said to Marguerite, " I was coming to see you. Something happened this morning and I thought I'd like to talk to Amedeo about it. I thought he might be able to advise me."

Marguerite nodded absently. She was looking nervous, indeed, almost haggard and far more distraught than the evening before.

" He's not at home this morning," she said. " He'd some business to see to. But I'll give him any message you like." She spoke listlessly, fidgeting with the glass of iced coffee.

" It's about Lester," Ruth said. " The police have been up at the villa, questioning us all and going through the place. You see, Lester wasn't killed in an accident. He was murdered."

Marguerite started. Yet the strange thing was that she did not really look shocked. It was more as if she had suddenly become confused. She looked muddled and lost.

" No, no," she muttered. Her breathing deepened and a flush mounted in her cheeks.

Stephen did not look shocked either. He did not even look surprised.

" Go on," he said to Ruth. But his eyes were on Marguerite's face in a glittering, absorbed stare.

Ruth found herself suddenly resenting that sharply. Until that moment she had never felt any conscious jealousy of Marguerite because of Stephen's interest in her, or recognised in herself any feelings about Stephen that could stimulate jealousy. Now, with fingers that all at once had become stiff and clumsy, she fumbled for her cigarettes while Stephen, surprisingly, produced a match.

"Lester was murdered," Ruth repeated. "He was shot through the head. He was dead before the car ran over him. It was run over him two or three times, to prevent identification, then his body was thrown into the ravine. I understand that there's no possible mistake about all that. But nothing else seems to be known. The police don't seem to know yet where Lester really was killed and if they suspect the reason or any particular person, they didn't show it."

"They questioned you, did they?" Marguerite tilted her glass of iced coffee this way and that, watching it carefully as the liquid swirled in the glass.

"Yes, and Madge and Cesare too," Ruth said.

"What sort of things did they ask you?"

"Oh, how long I'd worked for Lester and what did I know about his business and where was I during the afternoon and so on."

"And where were you?" Marguerite asked.

Ruth looked at her in surprise. "At your house, of course," she said.

Marguerite went on staring into her coffee. "Why, what were you doing there?"

For a moment Ruth thought that Marguerite must be suffering from shock far more than appeared.

"Waiting for you," Ruth said.

"But I was on the beach. Wasn't I, Stephen?"

"You were when I got there," he said.

"So why did you wait at the house?" Marguerite asked Ruth.

"Because you'd asked me to the house," Ruth said.

Marguerite shook her head slowly. "No," she said. She looked up from her glass of coffee into Stephen's eyes. "I asked you to meet me on the beach, didn't I?"

"Yes," he said.

"Of course," Marguerite went on, choosing her words thoughtfully, "if it'll help you, Ruth, if I say that I asked you to the house, I'll say it, but we'll have to work it out carefully between us, because somehow I don't think it will sound very convincing if I say that I asked you to meet me at the house and Stephen to meet me on the beach, both at the same time."

" But that's just what you must have done," Ruth said.

" No, but I'll say I did, if you like—if you think it will convince anybody."

Ruth was too amazed for the rage that was mounting inside her to have taken control of her yet and though her body had become tense, she could still speak fairly quietly and reasonably. " But you rang me up in the morning on purpose to remind me to come," she said, " and you left a note for me in the house, asking me to wait, which proves you were expecting me. I haven't the faintest idea what you're up to, Marguerite, whether it's just that the mere word murder has driven you out of your senses, or whether you yourself are more mixed up in all this——" She stopped, for a foot had just descended crushingly on one of her feet under the table.

" A note ? " Stephen said interestedly.

" I don't remember any note, my dears," Marguerite said. " But I could always write one, I suppose, if you think it would help. They couldn't prove it hadn't been written until to-day, could they ? Only let's not get too complicated. It never pays to get too complicated." She finished her coffee and stood up.

Ruth felt the explosion coming in herself, but the renewed pressure of Stephen's foot damped it.

Marguerite continued, " I must go home now. When I see Amedeo, I'll give him your message, Ruth. Of course, he'll do anything he can to help you. He's sure to know what you should do about a lawyer, or getting in touch with the consul, or whatever's best in the circumstances. And when you've had time to think things out, let me know what you want me to say about having asked you to the house when I wasn't there, only do remember that it really won't look too well if I try to provide alibis for too many people in different places at the same time."

With a special smile for Stephen, she walked away through the bright crowd strolling in the *piazza*.

X

" THE BITCH ! The double-faced, damned bitch ! " But
rather to her own amazement, Ruth said it softly instead of
shrieking it after the retreating figure. Then she turned on
Stephen. " It's all right, you can stop trying to break my
foot in two. But what was all that about ? "

" I think you need a drink before we proceed," he said,
" and I need another."

He waved at the waiter.

It took a little time to attract the waiter's attention. While
they were waiting, a little boy came up to their table and
shook a collecting-box under their noses. The collecting-box
had a picture of some saint on the side of it. Stephen pulled
some notes out of his pocket, chose one more or less at
random and pushed it into the box. The child thanked him
with quite excessive politeness and moved on to the next
table.

" That child dogs me wherever I go," Stephen said.
" He knows I always get muddled over the money and give
him more than I mean to."

Ruth had scarcely noticed the boy. During those few
minutes of waiting she had discovered that to be with
Stephen, following that first flare-up of jealousy inside
herself, felt quite different from how it had felt beforehand.

" And there's another with a pretty good racket," Stephen
added, pointing.

" What ? " Ruth asked vaguely.

" That boy with the tame budge in a cage," Stephen said.
" He'll be along presently. He makes the budge tell your
fortune. It's a neat little trick."

Ruth frowned. She imagined that Stephen was deliberately
trying to calm her down, afraid, perhaps, of an outburst that
would be overheard by people at tables nearby. But she did
not in the least want to be calmed down.

" What made you get her along here, too ? " she demanded.
" What was the point of that supposed to be ? "

"I didn't, believe it or not," Stephen said. "She got hold of me."

"You mean she saw you here, waiting?"

"No, she came round to my place, saying she wanted to talk to me, so I said all right, let's go and have a drink. That was in case you turned up here before I'd been able to get rid of her."

"And did she want to talk to you—I mean about all this affair?"

"Oh, yes. At least, I suppose that's what it was all about."

"What d'you mean?"

"Well, when you arrived, you broke in on a very earnest discussion of whether or not you and Ballard had been in love with one another. I told you she was rather strong on that idea, didn't I?"

Ruth felt a tingling in her cheeks. "And you think it's quite probable, I suppose?"

With an irritable frown, he answered, "How the hell is one to know about a thing like that, when half the time the people involved can't make up their minds about it? But I'll tell you something . . ."

"Well?"

"I've an idea—just an uncomfortable sort of idea—that you may find quite a number of people here going around with the same belief as Marguerite."

Ruth made no answer to that. As he said it, she had suddenly remembered the bewildering talk of Cesare in the garage, of his suggestion that Lester Ballard had, of course, been irresistible to Englishwomen, of his strange remarks about the heat of passion and the loss of reason.

Something in her face seemed to make an impression on Stephen, for in a different tone he added, "Look, I didn't say I did believe it. And anyway, what does it matter if I do or not?"

"I suppose what you've been tactfully leaving out," Ruth said, "is that people are going to go around now saying they always believed I was Lester's mistress, and that for a man to get shot by his mistress isn't an altogether unknown thing. Isn't that it?"

Stephen hesitated, " Well, I think it's what some people are going to believe."

" Including Marguerite ? "

" Oh, yes."

" Only she *doesn't* believe it."

" But I think she does, you know."

Ruth gave a decided shake of her head. " She doesn't believe it any more than she believes that she didn't ask me to her house yesterday, or that she didn't leave a note, asking me to wait. What I've only just discovered to-day is that for some mysterious reason, Marguerite hates me. I've always known she didn't care for me much, any more that I've really cared for her, but I never dreamt that she could be waiting for a chance, as she must have been, to do me some serious harm. She must hate me—simply hate me. Only why, unless she's mad ? I may not be anything very wonderful, but I'm not as awful as that, I know I'm not. So why on earth *should* she hate me so much ? "

" Possibly because she really does believe what you can't believe she does," Stephen said.

" That I was Lester's mistress ? But why should she think that ? Simply because we lived in the same house— and with Madge to keep an eye on us ! " Ruth could not help a scornful laugh.

" I rather think," he said, " that Marguerite believes the same thing of Madge."

" No, you're making that up ! "

" No, really. The eye of jealousy, and all that, you know. And Madge is a good-looking woman. Hadn't you noticed ? "

" So Lester was running a harem at the villa ? No!" Ruth laughed again. " But what d'you mean about jealousy ? You don't mean that Marguerite . . . ? " Pausing, she realised in a worried way that Stephen was looking at her with the rather angry expression that she had sometimes seen on his face, which made it look as if he had some personal grudge against her. " Well, what do you mean ? " she asked defensively.

He stood up.

" Let's go," he said. " I told you I'd something to show you. You'll have to come to my place, because, as I said, I couldn't tote it around. Actually, it explains a good many things, but I think you're going to find the explanation a bit of a shock. Not that that'll necessarily do you any harm."

Ruth did not rise. " Now, what's the matter ? " she asked. " What have I said ? "

He was counting greasy little notes on to the table.

" Come on," he said, " we'll talk when you've seen what I found."

" But why have you suddenly got so annoyed ? Is it because I thought for a moment you meant that Marguerite was jealous of me ? "

" She's blind, raving jealous—can't you see that ? Oh God, I simply don't know how to talk to a woman who hasn't got eyes in her head," Stephen said, " and who's going to need them as much as you are."

He would have walked away then from the table, only at that moment the boy whom he had pointed out to Ruth some minutes earlier, the boy who carried, slung over one shoulder, a small bird-cage with a budgerigar inside it, intercepted him. The boy was about thirteen. He was barefoot and wore patched blue cotton trousers that reached halfway down his calves, and a white cotton vest. He had a thin brown face and big, dark, melancholy eyes. Resolutely barring Stephen's way, he spoke in sing-song English.

" Hallo, mister, tell your fortune, tell the lady's fortune. You look here."

His hand groped inside the cage. Bringing out the budgerigar, he set it down on the edge of a tray fixed to the bottom of the cage and let the bird go. It gave a hop or two on the edge of the tray and ruffled its feathers, then pecked out of the tray a small paper envelope. It seemed to offer the envelope to Stephen.

The boy said, " Your fortune, mister. Take it and read it. Very interesting."

" Not now," Stephen said. " Another time." He managed to pass the boy.

Ruth followed Stephen.

He was living in an inn in a side street, the cheapest place that he had been able to find. It was some distance from the sea and very noisy, for life in that part of San Antioco went on until very late in the night on the doorsteps of all the houses, and began again very early in the morning.

Sometimes, Stephen had told Ruth, it seemed as if the people of that quarter never stopped shouting at one another, even to sleep. But the inn was clean and the family that owned it, which appeared to consist of one stout old woman and a limitless number of sons, daughters, cousins, aunts, uncles and even great-aunts and great-uncles, were kind and obliging, although the only efficient one amongst them was a boy of ten, who went about in a blue cotton livery, and who did all the heavy work, ordered his elder brothers and sisters about and stole Stephen's cigarettes.

Stephen took Ruth to his room, which was on the ground floor. It was a small room, furnished with a bed, an enormous rickety wardrobe, a table and a chair. Stephen's typewriter was on the table, together with a litter of papers. An open suitcase that Stephen had never quite finished unpacking, was on the floor. The window looked towards the side of a hill, terraced with vineyards.

Stephen went to the big wardrobe and opened it. This was not easy, for first the door stuck and on being tugged at, the whole wardrobe threatened to topple over, then the handle, a round wooden knob, came off in Stephen's hand and had to be twisted on to its pin again. When at last the door opened, it gave a loud, protesting creak, and revealed, so Ruth thought at first, that there was nothing inside the great dark cavern of the cupboard but one tweed jacket, suspended from a hook in the middle, so that it looked as if the coat had hanged itself.

But Stephen, reaching inside to the back of a shelf, brought out a bundle wrapped in newspaper.

" Lester's clothes," he said. " Though they aren't the most important thing. Still, there's something interesting about them. They've had every possible mark of identification cut out of them." He dropped the bundle on to the white cotton quilt on the bed and stripped away the folds of newspaper.

Lying in the nest of crumpled paper was a pair of blue cotton trousers and a checked shirt. Ruth looked sharply at Stephen.

He was staring at the bundle on the bed in utter bewilderment. " But these aren't the things I left here ! " Picking up the shirt, he fingered it feverishly.

Ruth took the shirt from him and shook it out. Stuck through one of the buttonholes was a faded sprig of bougainvillea. She dropped the shirt and turned on Stephen.

" Well now ? " she said.

He was still staring at the clothes as if they hypnotised him, but Ruth could see that he was thinking hard.

" Anyway, they didn't get what they were really looking for," he muttered. " But why leave these clothes here, even if they had to have the others ? "

" Perhaps because now you've got the job of getting rid of them," Ruth said.

" Is that important ? "

" Well, I think they're the clothes of the other man who was murdered—the one who was found in Lester's clothes."

" Why d'you think so ? " His voice had dropped to a whisper. " Have you seen them before ? "

" Yes." Ruth was whispering, too. " There was a man at the villa yesterday morning. He was wearing these clothes. I remember that little bit of bougainvillea. He turned up soon after breakfast and sat down on the wall beside the road to wait. He was still there when we came back from the beach."

" I didn't see anyone," Stephen said.

" No, I don't mean he was still sitting on the wall, but he was somewhere around, because when we started walking down the hill I happened to look back and he was there again."

Stephen gave her a thoughtful look.

" I didn't see him," he repeated. Picking up the shirt once more, he looked at it closely. " Still, it looks as if you're right, at least in part. See those stains ? "

They were bloodstains. The back of the shirt was dark and stiff with them.

" And someone came here this morning while I was in the *piazza*," he went on, " and took away the clothes Ballard was wearing when he was killed, leaving these instead. I'll ask the people here if they saw anyone, but it would be easy to get in from the back without being seen. The question is, who knew I was going to be out ? "

" I did," Ruth said.

" Did you tell anyone you were meeting me in the *piazza* ? "

" No, I told Cesare I was going to the Ranzis."

" Of course, Marguerite knew. She could have come here after she left us."

" Only she wasn't carrying anything. If she'd come straight here, she'd have had to have this bundle with her."

" That's true." He began to roll the clothes up in the folds of newspaper.

" It may be that someone was watching and saw you go out," Ruth said, " or else that someone just came on chance, with a reasonable excuse ready if they happened to find you."

" Or it may be that Marguerite was sent to get me out of the way."

" *Sent ?* You don't mean—by Amedeo ? "

" I don't know whom I mean." Stephen put the bundle back on the shelf in the cavernous wardrobe and laboured to close the door again. " But whoever it was, not having got what he wanted, I suppose he'll be back again. We'd better do a little careful thinking, you and I, because it looks as if life is going to get very uncomfortable."

" If you'd just get on and tell me what he really came for . . ."

" This." Stephen put a hand into a pocket of the jacket he was wearing and brought out a packet. " You'll see when you take a look at what's there that I couldn't very well show it to you in a public place. Two of these documents are rather recognisable, even at a distance, and they might be thought queer things for us to be studying carefully."

Ruth saw at once what he meant. The two documents in question were British passports.

She looked at the names on the outside. The passports belonged to a Mr. and Mrs. Danbury. With the passports were a cheque book, a quantity of bank-notes, British and Italian, a small red note-book and two steamship tickets. The tickets were for the passage from Naples to Buenos Aires.

Ruth was looking at the tickets when Stephen said, " Look inside the passports."

She put the other things down and opened the passports. At once she realised why Stephen was watching her with such a strained air of suspense. For the face that looked at her out of the passport of Mr. Nigel Porter Danbury,

electrical engineer, was unquestionably that of Lester
Ballard, while as unquestionably, the face that was said to
belong to Mrs. Mildred Ann Danbury, housewife, was that
of Marguerite Ranzi.

XI

RUTH LOOKED up at Stephen.

" Lester and Marguerite. . . . So that *was* what you
meant when you were talking about her jealousy."

" Of course it was," he said impatiently. His face had
flushed and his voice had a nervous note of harshness in it.

Ruth wondered what this discovery had meant to him.
He was more than half in love with Marguerite himself, she
was sure.

" But that doesn't make sense," she said. " Because if
she and Lester were going away together, why should she
bother with being jealous of me ? "

" Because they *haven't* gone away together," Stephen said,
fretting at her slowness. " Don't you see, from Marguerite's
angle, it must look as if she's just been left flat by Lester.
He's gone off without her, that's what she thinks. She isn't
to know that he never went either."

" But she does know he's dead," Ruth said. " She knows
—that's to say, she thinks—that he's the one who was found
in the ravine."

" No, she doesn't."

Ruth looked at him helplessly. " Well, I don't understand."

He started walking up and down the small room. There
was something feverish in his movements and his breathing
was rapid.

" It looks as if you don't recognise a murderess when you
see one," he said. " I can't say I did, either, till the evidence
was pushed under my nose. Quite a nice woman, I thought.
Nice looking, quite amusing, easy to get along with. She
made quite a difference to San Antioco for a little while.
Yet the dear creature turns out to be a cold-blooded
murderess. How's that for a joke on us all ? "

" Don't," Ruth said. " And I still don't understand."

He came to a stop, facing her, and began to talk, making quick little emphatic gestures with his hands, as if to hammer home his points to someone particularly slow-witted.

" Look, this is what happened—it's all quite simple, really. She and Ballard wanted to go off together. So they decided to do a disappearing act. They got a couple of fake passports, they got tickets to South America. But they thought they'd like to leave things nice and tidy, with a dead Ballard on hand to stop any hue and cry. So they decided to get hold of a corpse. This man you say you saw at the villa, perhaps that's who it was. Ballard had fixed it for him to come to the villa that day, choosing the day, you notice, when the Gargiulos would be away in Naples. But you had to be got out of the way too, so Marguerite invited you to visit her, even ringing you up again on the morning of the day when the murder was to happen, to make sure you wouldn't forget the arrangement. But then she herself took her car, left it at the top of the path down to the cove and went and spent the whole afternoon on the rocks down there, where a lot of people could see her. There wasn't to be any doubt at all that she had an alibi for the time of the murder. But besides that, I think there was another reason why she couldn't simply stay at home and spend the afternoon with you. I think it was her car that Ballard was going to get away in. It had to be left near his villa so that when he'd shot this other man, dressed him up in his own clothes, driven him up the mountain road, run over him and dumped him in the ravine, Ballard had a car to get away in. He couldn't go in his own, because that had to be left in the garage in the normal way. Things were supposed to look, you see, as if he'd come home and then simply taken his favourite walk up the mountain road and been run down by a hit-and-run driver. So it was imperative that his own car should be left in the garage. But Marguerite could have her car stolen without its being connected with him. I'm pretty sure that's the real reason why she couldn't keep her appointment with you—and also why she was so anxious that I should go swimming with her. I was to come up from the cove with her and be a witness to the fact that her car had been stolen. As things turned out, of course, I was a witness to her finding it still there—

and I did think at the time that her behaviour just then was a little odd. People don't usually mind finding their cars where they left them. What she didn't know was that just when Ballard was ready to leave the villa, someone else took a hand in things and murdered him. And she still doesn't know it. She thinks that Ballard didn't use her car because he'd prepared some other method of getting away. She thinks he's gone off and left her."

"Poor Marguerite." Ruth said it without irony, thinking that if all this was true, Marguerite's load of misery that morning must be dreadful beyond imagination. " I suppose he was going to send her a message from somewhere, telling her where to join him, and he hasn't, and that's all she knows."

After that Ruth sat for some moments without speaking, gazing past Stephen at the window and the hillside, striped with its vineyards.

" No," she said suddenly. " There are all sorts of things the matter with that."

" What ? " Stephen asked.

" Well, it isn't a crime if two people want to go away together, even if one of them is married to someone else. Nobody can stop them if they've made up their minds to do it. They've no need to fake disappearances and pretend to be dead and even commit murder to support the story. They can simply pack their suitcases and go. Then there's another thing—money. So far as I've ever heard, neither Marguerite nor Lester had any money outside of Italy and you can't take much money out of Italy nowadays. So what were they going to use for money in South America ? I don't think they were people who'd willingly embrace poverty, even for love."

" We don't know enough yet," Stephen said. " We'll find an explanation of all that if we go on looking."

" But how can we go on looking ? We did such mad things yesterday that now we daren't go to anyone with this information we've got."

" I'm not sure that they were so mad. But there's something you've got to tell me, Ruth."

" There's something you've got to tell me ! "

" What's that ? "

"Were you at the villa yesterday afternoon—before you walked in and found me with Lester?"

"No. Did somebody tell you I was?"

"No."

"Then what makes you think I might have been?"

He was looking at her intently. Ruth did not altogether like the look.

"I know it'll sound stupid," she said, "but it's because of a box of matches. I found a box of matches on the table on the terrace when I got back from the Ranzis' house. You're always leaving matches about."

"Is that all?"

She nodded.

He laughed but his eyes were not amused. "Don't you remember that I sat on the terrace for a while in the morning while you were upstairs, changing?"

"Yes, I remember that," she said. "But you had matches at lunch. It was you who lighted our cigarettes."

"If you say so. You seem to have a better memory for details than I have."

"In this case, at any rate."

He laughed again. "And on the evidence of a box of matches, you think I really know more about Ballard's murder than I've told you?"

"I don't know what to think."

"Nor do I, by God!" He sat down suddenly on the edge of the bed. The antagonism went out of his manner. "I wonder if this damned box of matches is going to lead to trouble between us—because the explanation's very simple and yet it's just the sort of thing that's awfully hard to make sound convincing to anyone but oneself. The fact is, I'm just as likely to have two or three boxes of matches in various pockets as I am to have none. If, as you say, I left one on the terrace in the morning and yet had another at lunch, it's just that I must have started out that day with at least two. Now does that explanation make you feel reasonably happy or does it just make you feel certain I'm a glib but not very effective liar?"

Ruth wished that she could have said definitely which of these things she felt. She said, "At least I do see that that's quite in character."

" Character ! " Stephen said. " That's dangerous ground.
It's a subject that embarrasses me deeply at the moment.
I used to think I was a wonderful judge of character and that
that was why I ought to stop being a physical chemist and
write novels. Did you know that was my history ? Have I
mentioned that that's how I got to be in this situation ? And
if you say it serves me right, I shan't take it ill—because I'm
beginning to think that half the attraction of writing novels
is that, having invented the characters, one can claim to
understand them at least half-way. But the people I actually
know, the Marguerite Ranzis, the Ruth Seabrights. . . ."

Ruth thought uneasily that he was talking a great deal.

" You said there was something you wanted me to tell
you," she said.

" Yes—though that's a question of character, too, so after
all, why ask it ? You'll only give me the same sort of answer
that I gave you about the match-box."

" I think I believe you about the match-box," she said.

His eyes searched hers. " Yes—until some other odd
thing makes you suspicious, when what I told you won't
mean a thing any more."

" All the same, go on and ask what you want to."

" All right." But he seemed to have to consider how to
put his question. While he hesitated, he fiddled with
Marguerite's forged passport. Then he spoke hurriedly. " I
don't really believe any more that you killed Ballard. For a
little while yesterday I thought so. I thought I'd almost
caught you in the act. Still, if you didn't, why did you let
me hide the body ? Why did you identify that second man
as Ballard ? Because, you see, if you're innocent, those
things aren't in character. You're the sort of person who's
normally honest and who always feels safest telling the truth.
You've an ingrained habit of telling the truth and you know
that people recognise that and believe you. So even when
the truth looks rather dangerous, you're less afraid of it
than of being entangled in lies. Truth will prevail, and so on.
You do believe that. Now I'm not like that at all. I'm dis-
trustful of people, so I lie to them easily, and I think too
fast for my own good, making myself think I see ways of
dodging around problems so that I won't have to face them.
If I'd been the person who identified that second man as

Ballard, and who even now doesn't seem to be wondering if it mightn't be a good thing to go to the police and tell them that they've two dead bodies on their hands, there'd be nothing peculiar about it. It's the sort of thing I do. But not you. You'd have to have some very good reason for it. And what I want to know is—what is that reason ? "

The answer should have been very simple. She needed to say only one word—Nicky. She wanted to say it. She wanted intensely just then to put herself completely into Stephen's hands. She had become so confused in her feelings about him that the thought of telling him the truth of what she had seen that afternoon, before he had walked in and found her, seemed to promise a simplification of everything, but particularly of what he meant to her himself. A day or so ago she would have sworn that she did not even find him attractive, and even now she saw that he did not fit in any way with any ideas that she had ever had as to what an attractive man should be like. Yet simply being near to him was producing a tension in her that made it almost impossible for her to go on thinking clearly.

Restlessly she turned away so that she did not have to look at him sitting there, holding Marguerite's forged passport.

There was as much need as before for her to think clearly. Stephen had never had any particular liking for Nicky. He had not seemed to be much impressed by her reasons for devoting herself to the boy, and though he seemed ready to take big risks on her account, there was not much likelihood that he would take such risks for Nicky. In fact, his very desire to protect her might turn him against Nicky.

Besides, she had to remember that the risks he was taking might not be on her account at all.

" I'm afraid you've got me all wrong, Stephen." She turned again to face him. " I'm certainly not honest and I'm very frightened. There's no need for you to hunt for any other reason."

He said nothing, seeming to be waiting for her to add something.

" Really and truly," she said. " I'm horribly frightened. Don't you believe it ? "

" Oh, yes, I believe that—I'm horribly frightened, too."

But he said it in a discouraged tone, almost as if he had suddenly become bored by the whole matter. Flipping over the pages of the passport in his hand he said vaguely, " I wonder how one gets hold of a thing like this when one happens to want one. I shouldn't have the faintest idea how to set about it. I suppose Ballard must have had contacts." He tossed the passport aside and picked up the red note-book. " You haven't looked at this yet." He held it out to Ruth.

She took the note-book from him. She was half disappointed that he had dropped his questioning so easily and she found herself wanting to go on explaining and justifying what she had done. Opening the note-book, she tried to concentrate on it.

It was an address-book, full of names and addresses and telephone numbers, written in Lester Ballard's small, neat handwriting. Most of the names and addresses were familiar to Ruth. They were of Lester Ballard's friends in San Antioco and his business associates in other parts of Italy. A few of the addresses were in England. Some were in the United States. Among these Ruth recognised the names of some of Lester Ballard's customers. But there was nothing that struck her as being of particular interest.

" Look on the last page," Stephen said.

She looked. The last page was blank, except for a number—B.A. 34.77429.

" What does it mean ? " she asked.

" I don't know," Stephen said, " but I've got a queer feeling about it. I've got a feeling that whoever searched my room this morning was after that number, not the passports. And that's what they'll come after again."

" But what I can't understand is, how did they know you had it ? " Ruth said. " How did they know you'd got Lester's clothes ? "

" That's easy," Stephen said. " There was someone else at the villa yesterday afternoon while we were talking to the police and while I was stripping the body and cleaning up, someone who watched and listened and who knows just what we've done."

She stared at him blankly. " But who ? "

" The murderer, of course," he answered.

XII

SHE KNEW that he was wrong. She had seen the murderer, blood-smeared and terror-struck by his own act, go shooting down the hill on his bicycle to San Antioco. Besides that, there had been some other important error in Stephen's explanation. There had been some mistake in it that she ought to have recognised while he was speaking. Possibly this thing that he had just said was connected with it. Somebody besides Nicky and herself must have been in the house. That seemed clear. But thinking about that, her dissatisfaction with Stephen's explanation remained.

" Well, what are we going to do ? " she asked hopelessly.

" Wait and see, I suppose," Stephen said.

" For what ? "

" For this beggar to come after this note-book again."

" And then you catch hold of him and say, ' You're the murderer,' and hope you survive the experience ? "

" It doesn't sound particularly attractive, does it ? " He gave a grin. " If I'd a better plan to offer, I would. But it seems to me that unless we broadcast the fact that I've got rid of these documents somehow, which means letting the police in on the fact that I've had them, this character is going to come after me anyhow. I can't think of any way of avoiding him except doing a bolt."

" Then why not do a bolt ? "

" That's what I've been asking myself ever since I unrolled that bundle and realised what had happened," he said. " Why not do a bolt ? You know, it must be awfully nice to be a hero and not even ask oneself questions like that. But I'm not one. I never was one. You've got yourself a very frightened accomplice, Ruth. If you can find a better one, employ him promptly." While he was speaking, he had taken the red note-book from her and was looking frowningly at the number on the last page.

" Well, why don't you go ? " Ruth said.

" For reasons, various. Got a match ? " He had just torn the last page out of the note-book.

She exclaimed quickly, " What are you going to do ? You're not going to burn that ! The number may be important."

" It's all right," he said. " I've got a very good memory for numbers. For names my mind's like a leaky sieve, but numbers stick."

Ruth found a match-box in her bag and handed it to him. Striking a match, he held it to a corner of the page that he had torn out of the book, then when the paper had been completely consumed, he took a pencil out of his pocket and wrote on the page that was now the last in the book the number—B.A. 33.71937.

" Now I can afford to let them take it from me without putting up a struggle, which suits my nature," he said.

" If you're right that the number was what they were after."

He gave her a dubious look. " You think I ought to put up a struggle, just in case ? Not me, if I can help it. I'm very peaceable and cautious."

She burst out laughing. " You may or may not be a hero —on our slight acquaintance, I wouldn't presume to offer an opinion—but I think you're the most crazily reckless person I've ever known. From the time that you moved the couch. . . ."

" No. I've an active but indisciplined sense of self-preservation, that's all. Now don't you think perhaps you'd better be going home ? It's probable that the police are keeping an eye on you and we don't want them to start getting the wrong ideas."

" Are you going to take reasonable care of yourself ? " she asked uneasily.

" Oh, yes, I'll stick to public places and avoid dark alleys."

They went out together.

As they reached the street, something exploded near them. Ruth jumped and clutched Stephen's arm. But as another explosion followed the first, she let go of him and laughed self-consciously.

" A *fiesta*," she said.

" That's all," Stephen said.

Several more bangs, sounding like anti-aircraft fire,

followed the first two. Out of the clear sky, some tatters of dirty paper drifted downwards. At the end of the street, in a small square with a few agaves in a plot in the centre, some young men were letting off rockets.

Presently there were more explosions in other parts of the town. Little puffs of smoke appeared in the sky and released torn scraps of dirty paper.

" How they love noise," Stephen said. " Just noise, from their sopranos to their motor-bicycles."

" I suppose I've got used to it," Ruth said. " Usually I don't notice it. All the same, to-day I don't like it."

She stepped out into the street. " Remember," she added, " no dark alleys."

Stephen made a gesture of obedience, and went back into the inn.

When Ruth reached the villa there was still, as she had expected, no news of Nicky. Madge had come to the door to meet her and when Ruth asked her if she was feeling better now, shrugged her shoulders and said it didn't matter how she felt. She did not look at all unwell, but there was a look of sullen self-pity on her face. As if it were a fact of no importance, she told Ruth that a man had come to see her, and not bothering even to say who the man was, went back to the kitchen.

Ruth knew Madge in these moods and had given up struggling against them. The only thing to do was to leave her alone until the mood had passed off. Even Lester Ballard had known this. Though he had always loved to tease anyone whom he had recognised as being in a responsively nervous state, he had never risked it with Madge. She could silence him without saying anything or doing anything but turning her brooding stare on him for a moment. Ruth, who believed that most of Madge's bad moods were caused by Cesare, the only person who appeared to be completely insensitive to them, wondered what he had been doing this morning to upset her so much.

Going to the drawing-room, Ruth expected to find that the man who had come to see her was one of the police officers, but as she came into the room, an old, bald-headed man with pince-nez and a crumpled linen suit got uncertainly

to his feet. It was Luigi Sebastiano, the manager of Lester
Ballard's antique shop in Naples.

She could see that he was very agitated and when he
shook her hand, she could feel that his was trembling. It
was very sweaty too and sweat stood out in beads all over his
bald, yellow forehead.

" Is it true ? " he asked quaveringly. " Is it true, this
terrible thing they've told me, that the boy has killed his
father ? "

" Sit down, Signor Sebastiano, please sit down, you don't
look well," she said and pulled a chair forward for him.

" But is it true ? " He would not let go of her hand.
" It isn't true, is it ? I shall tell them myself that it isn't
true."

" Who told you it was true ? " she asked.

To her relief he sank into the chair. " I'm all right, I'm
quite all right," he assured her, breathing heavily. " But it's
the shock. I can't believe it's true. You don't believe it's
true, do you ? "

" No," Ruth said, " I don't believe it." She sat down too,
suddenly feeling so exhausted that she wanted to burst
into tears. She had nothing against the old man, she had
never heard anything but good of him and on the few
occasions when they had met he had been charming and
kind to her. But to have to cope with him then was almost
more than she could bear. " Can't I fetch you something
to drink ? " she suggested. " An iced drink or some coffee."

" No, no, thank you, I'm very well," he said. " Please
don't trouble yourself. But tell me about this terrible
thing. What's happened to the boy ? Is it true that he's
run away ? "

" I'm afraid so."

" But why ? Nicky's a good boy. We're all his friends.
Why should he run away from us ? "

" I wish I knew," Ruth said with a heavy sigh.

" He couldn't have killed his father," Sebastiano said.
" If Signor Ballard was murdered, as they've been telling me,
then it wasn't Nicky who did it."

" But who told you it was ? " she asked. " Surely not the
police ? "

" No, not directly. But they asked me so many questions

about him. . . . They seemed to think I might know where he'd gone. We were good friends, of course, he and I. He liked me to show him the beautiful things we have and explain them to him. He was very sensitive to beautiful things, much more than his father. Signor Ballard understood commercial values, but for the form, for the craftsmanship, for the noble history of a piece of furniture, for the wonderful texture of rare glazes, he cared very little. But Nicky has these things. He is like his grandfather, who taught me all that I know. Nicky is like his mother, too. You never knew her, did you ? No, of course not. I knew her from the time when she was a child. She was a very sweet and good woman, beautiful in the way that the boy is beautiful, and, like him, she had always a core of unhappiness in her. It was as if she had been born with a pain in her heart for which there was no cure. That kind of woman very often marries a bad man, you know. It is as if she needs pain to go on living. So she loves passionately but only where it can do her harm."

" Then you think that Signor Ballard was a bad man ? "

" Yes, he was a bad man."

" In what way ? " Ruth spoke more sharply than she had meant to, for the firmness in his quavering voice had startled her.

The old man looked confused. Taking off his pince-nez, he rubbed first one eye, then the other, as if they had grit in them.

" I'm sorry—he's dead," he mumbled. " I should not have spoken so. Perhaps you cared for him."

" No, I thought he was a bad man too," Ruth said. " I thought that he was cruel and neglectful to Nicky. But I thought, from the way you said it, that you might have some other reason for calling him a bad man."

Sebastiano polished his glasses carefully, then clipped them on to his nose again. His eyes, reddened by rubbing, regarded her warily.

" I've known for a long time that he was a bad man, a very bad man, a criminal," he said at last. " I could have gone to the police about it long ago. But I was frightened. I ought to have gone, I know it, and now I would give anything to be able to think that I had done my duty at the right time. But I was too frightened."

" Frightened of Lester Ballard ? " she asked. " Did he threaten you in some way ? "

" Oh, no, he never even knew what I knew. He thought I was old and blind and foolish, which was what he wanted, and so he treated me very well and let me keep my job. No, it was of losing my job that I was frightened. I'm old, my heart is bad, I have very little money. And it is the easiest thing in the world to shut one's eyes, do you know that ? All over the world people do it all the time, quite good people. They shut their eyes to crimes that disgust and enrage them whenever they stop to think about them for a moment, yet they do not even sleep badly at night. Occasionally I have slept badly, thinking about my cowardice, but not very often. I have been much more troubled by the fear that someone would find out how much I knew—the police, perhaps, or Signor Ballard. Either would have been fatal to me. For the police would rightly have called me an accessory to the crime, while Signor Ballard—I think perhaps he would have had me killed."

" But this crime,—what was it ? " Ruth asked excitedly.

" He was a receiver of stolen goods."

" Oh . . . Oh, I see ! "

Her first thought was to get hold of Stephen immediately, for this was something that he ought to hear at once. But she could not telephone while Sebastiano was in the room.

" Did he deal in jewels ? " she asked.

He looked at her alertly. " How did you know that ? It used to be mostly in pictures, but lately it has been in precious stones of all kinds. But how did you know ? "

" The police asked me if he dealt in jewels," she said. " They asked it rather insistently. I didn't think much about it at the time."

" So they've become suspicious." He sat staring at her, but looking right through her. " I decided this morning to go to them in any case, because I'm sure that Nicky had nothing to do with his father's death. It was a gang-murder. Signor Ballard had somehow offended the head of the gang, the man who was really at the top. I'm certain that's what happened."

" Then wasn't Lester Ballard the head ? "

" Oh, no. His only use to the gang was that he was the

owner of a well-known business with a fine reputation. It was a reputation that had taken two generations to create. Signora Ballard's father and grandfather had built it up by their scrupulousness and their wide knowledge and their integrity. Who could suspect such a place of having become a rendezvous for thieves, the property of a cheap crook? Not that it has any more the reputation that it once had. Sometimes when I've stood looking around me in the shop at the fake things on show there now, d'you know, I've actually found tears in my eyes. But still I was frightened, too frightened to do anything."

" But who is this boss? " Ruth asked.

" I don't know. I don't think he ever came to the shop, but I think Signor Ballard was often in communication with him. I've heard him speak of him to the men who came there, giving them orders. I think Signor Ballard was scared of him. Sometimes he'd be in a rage with everyone because the boss had abused him for some mistake."

" And you think this boss murdered him? "

" Or had him murdered by someone else in the gang. I think perhaps Signor Ballard had made some mistake that endangered them all and so was put out of the way. And I'll tell you what else I think.' Sebastiano leant towards her and stubbed at her arm with a thick, shaky finger. " I think Nicky saw it happen and that's why he's run away. I don't think he's hiding from the police, I think he's hiding from the gang. And I hope he remains in hiding because if he came back, I think they would kill him at sight."

Ruth got up abruptly and walked across the room. Going to the window, she leant against its frame, and listened to the sound of the rockets that were being let off in San Antioco. The noise of them would go on all day, increasing towards the evening, when a procession of some sort, with religious images carried on the shoulders of the people, would wend its way, singing, through the town. This happened so often that usually, as Ruth had told Stephen, she scarcely noticed it. But to-day the noise of each explosion in the distance jabbed at her nerves.

She realised that Sebastiano believed that the dead man found beside the mountain road was Lester Ballard. It was of that murder that he was thinking. He did not know that there had been another murder here in this room, and that she had seen Nicky rush from the room, with blood on his face and his shirt and with something in his hand, a thing that probably had just been used to batter a man to death. What the old man had told her might have something to do with Lester Ballard's desire to disappear from San Antioco, but it had no bearing on his murder.

She turned back to face the old man.

" What are you going to do about it ? " she asked.

He twisted his hands together. " I must go to the police, mustn't I ? There's no way out of it now. I care very much for that boy. His mother and all his people have been very good to me. It leaves me under an obligation from which I hope I shall not shrink."

" What will happen to you ? "

" Who knows ? " He lifted his shoulders. " I think I have more to fear now from my bad heart than from a prison sentence. Whether that sentence is long or short will not make much difference to me."

" Don't you think perhaps that if what you tell them helps them to catch a murderer, they won't be very severe with you ? "

" Perhaps. You are kind to suggest it."

" But why did you come and tell me all this, Signor Sebastiano ? "

" Because you care for the boy. I hoped to help set your mind at rest."

" That was very good of you."

" And he cares for you very much." Putting his hands on the arms of his chair, he pushed himself laboriously to his feet. " When all this is over, I hope you will not leave him immediately. I know that you will have to think of your own future, but I hope that you will find that you can think of him as well. He is not a murderer. You have no need to fear that. After all, the murderer drove a car, didn't he ? He took the body up the mountain road by car. And we all know that Nicky could not drive a car." He held out his hand to her.

At that moment they both heard someone walking quickly across the terrace.

Sebastiano's hand dropped to his side. As he looked

anxiously towards the window, a tall shadow passed it, then the voice of Amedeo Ranzi was heard from the door.

" May I come in, Ruth ? "

Following his words, Ranzi came in. In surprise he exclaimed, " Signor Sebastiano ! "

The two men shook hands formally.

" I'm just leaving, Signor Ranzi," the old man said. His manner had immediately become a little obsequious. " I came to offer my condolences and any help that I am able to give."

" But please don't hurry on my account," Ranzi said. " I have nothing private or urgent to say to Miss Seabright. Please don't let me hasten your departure."

" Not at all, not at all, I was just going in any case." Sebastiano again held out his hand to Ruth.

As she took it, Ranzi asked, " Are you going back to Naples, Signor Sebastiano ? I have my car here. If you'll wait a few minutes, I'll drive you to the station."

The old man replied that that was very kind. Ruth saw that he would have preferred to refuse the offer, but that he did not know how to do so without letting Ranzi discover that he had business with the police in San Antioco.

" Let me take you to my car now," Ranzi said, " then if you won't mind waiting for just a few minutes while I talk to Miss Seabright. . . ."

The two men went out together. Ruth, waiting, wondered what had brought Ranzi. For in spite of what he had said, it obviously was something both private and urgent.

After a minute or two he returned. He came in hurriedly and looked as if he were about to start speaking immediately. But then he seemed to forget what he had been about to say and stood looking at Ruth perplexedly, so that she felt that he was expecting her to find his words for him.

" Well ? " she said.

He started and frowned. Then, as he drew himself up. something haughty and formidable appeared in his manner.

" My wife tells me that she saw you this morning," he said. " She tells me that you insisted that she had invited you to our house yesterday afternoon and then had failed to keep her appointment with you. From the questions that the police have put to me, I understand that you told the same story to them. This was very foolish of you. Unwilling as we both are to say or do anything that could harm you in any way, you must realise that you cannot expect us to lie on your account. It would have been much wiser on your part to tell the truth, whatever it was." He paused, then in a hoarser voice, repeated, " *Whatever it was !* "

XIII

So HE KNOWS, Ruth thought. He knows about Marguerite and Lester.

She could not have given her reason for leaping to this conclusion. But in Ranzi's face and tone of voice there was something that told her that he was deliberately acting a part. It told her also that he was acting half-heartedly. He did not like the line that he had taken. He had not enjoyed saying what he had said. But if Ruth or his wife had to be sacrificed, it would not be his wife.

Ruth felt surprisingly little anger. She almost wished that she had some idea of how to penetrate the manner that had always intimidated her and to assure him that he had her sympathy. Not that he would have accepted it or responded to it with anything but increased hauteur and great resentment.

But how much, she wondered, did he actually know and how much had he merely guessed ? Did he know that Marguerite had meant to leave him for Lester Ballard ? Did he know of Lester Ballard's criminal activities in Naples ? Did he know that Marguerite had almost certainly helped Lester to carry out a murder ? Did he realise that it was her own guilt that she was trying to shift on to Ruth ? Or had he merely perceived that Marguerite had been in love with Lester and now needed his help in preventing her affair with him being brought to light during the police investigation ?

Ruth did not realise how long she had remained silent while these questions passed through her mind. She had stood there looking at Ranzi in quiet thoughtfulness. It was only when she saw the perplexity in his eyes at this strange response of hers to his speech, that it occurred to her that she ought to say something.

She said, "Yes, I see what you mean." Then she was sorry that she had said it, since the words were so obviously caustic.

"Believe me," Ranzi said, "I do not want to harm you."

"No, I think I understand that," she said.

"You will find it safest in the end to stick to the truth."

"In other words, I must think of some other story," she said.

"There should, if possible, be some support for it."

"On which I can rely."

He nodded gravely, without appearing to notice any irony in the words.

"Isn't there anyone who saw you during the afternoon?" he asked. "Isn't there anyone who can say that you could not have been here at the time of the murder?"

"Here?" Ruth said. "Have they decided that the murder was done here? I wonder how they arrived at that."

His sallow face flushed. He had made a blunder.

"It's you who seem very anxious to prove that you couldn't have been here," he said. "Well, did nobody see you? Isn't there anyone who can corroborate the fact that you were absent?"

Ruth saw the trap and decided not to step into it. Although she had some sympathy for Ranzi and some admiration for his blind loyalty to his wife, she saw no reason why she should play into his hands. If he wanted to find out whether or not there was anyone who knew that Marguerite had telephoned to her in the morning before the murder, or had seen Ruth enter or leave the Ranzi's house in San Antioco, she herself was not going to help him to the answer.

"I'll think it over," she said. "Perhaps there was some-one. Perhaps——" A thought had just struck her and now that it had done so, she could not imagine why it had not come to her before. Perhaps someone had heard the tele-phone ring that morning and had heard her talking to Marguerite. Perhaps Nicky had heard it.

However, she did not know for certain whether or not Nicky had still been in the house when the telephone rang, and even if he had, he could have heard only her end of the conversation.

Ranzi had been watching her face.

"You've thought of something ?" he said.

She believed that she caught a sound of hope in the words. It seemed almost that Ranzi wanted her to be able to defeat his treachery to her. But she shrugged her shoulders.

"I'm not sure," she said.

"Well, I must not keep Signor Sebastiano waiting any longer," Ranzi said. "This is all a great misfortune for him, because I suppose the stock will be sold up and the shop closed and he will find himself unemployed. He is a well-known man in his line, of course. He has a wide knowledge and a very good reputation. But in these difficult times a man as old and sick as he is will not be much in demand. I hope he has savings."

He gave a stiff little bow and turned to go. Ruth was glad that he had not offered to shake hands with her, as he usually did, and she was glad when she heard the car drive away. The sense of the strain between them had been increasing with each thing that was said, and each moment it had felt harder to keep her voice steady.

Perhaps he had scared her far more than she realised, for as soon as he had gone, she started to tremble violently. She was afraid that she was going to start crying and had a horrible feeling that she would actually like to shout and scream.

In a hurry she went to the cupboard in the corner, where Lester Ballard had kept his drinks and poured out a glass of brandy. At that moment Madge came into the room.

"I wouldn't mind some of that myself," she said. "I think I'll join you."

Taking the decanter from Ruth, she reached into the cupboard for a glass and helped herself.

"So it's really got you at last," she went on. "I've been wondering how long it'd be before you started to crack. What's old Ranzi been saying to upset you so ? Whatever it was, love, I shouldn't worry." Madge's bad mood appeared to be past its worst. Her manner was almost back to its normal abrupt friendliness. "That man's got

only one idea in his head and that's that precious wife of his.
Queer the way some women can pull it off, isn't it? She's
nothing but a tart and he knows it and yet he'll stand by
her whatever she gets up to. Wish I knew how it was
done."

" You stand a good deal yourself from Cesare, don't you?"
Ruth said, sitting down, leaning back and feeling the brandy
begin to work comfortingly on her nerves. " Speaking as
an outsider, it seems to me that marriage does queer things
to people."

Madge laughed shortly. She dropped into a chair too and
took a good-sized gulp from her glass. As she did so, it
occurred to Ruth that in spite of Madge's power over
everyone at the villa, this was the first time that she had seen
her sitting down in that room.

" It's a habit you get into," Madge said. She started
scratching some of the mosquito bites on her ankles. " If
it wasn't a habit, I'd have left Cesare long ago. He's a lazy,
good-for-nothing rat who'd never trouble to earn a penny on
my account and who isn't faithful to me. But I've left it a
bit late for starting all over again. Five years ago I might
have made up my mind to it, but now it doesn't seem
worth the trouble."

Ruth looked at her wonderingly. " But aren't you awfully
unhappy?"

" Who isn't, love? You look around you and see if you
can pick out anyone you can really call happy. Can you do
it?"

" I'm sure I can—well, reasonably happy, at any rate,"
Ruth said.

" Probably that just means you don't know them very well.
Take this lot here, for instance—Ballard and the Ranzis and
you and me. . . . Up to a few days ago, wouldn't you have
said we were all reasonably happy? And now think what
you've started to find out about us all. It doesn't look the
same, does it? Mind you, I could have told you a lot of it
ages ago, but then I've got a way of noticing things and I'm
not put off by unpleasant facts. I've seen too many of them.
No, the great thing is, when you've got used to a thing, stick
to it. You know that you can stand it and you may not be
able to stand what you'd get instead if you changed. But

perhaps you're too young still to know what I'm talking about."

Ruth was thinking. "Then you heard most of that conversation that I had just now with Mr. Ranzi?"

"That's right," Madge said. "I've always heard a lot of things that went on in this house."

"What did you make of it, then—of what he said to me about my going to their house?"

"Well, love, if I had to choose whom I was to believe about something, you or that Ranzi woman, I'd choose you every time."

"That's something, at any rate."

"But that doesn't mean everyone else will do the same. It's my own belief that you're in a nasty position and that it's in certain people's interests to keep you there."

"You mean the Ranzis?" Ruth was beginning to wonder how much Madge really knew. Was it possible, for instance, that she knew, not merely of the affair between Marguerite and Lester, but that they had been planning to disappear together?

Madge shrugged her shoulders. "They must be mixed up in it somehow or they wouldn't be so anxious to land you in a mess. They must be scared of something coming out, though from what I hear Mrs. Ranzi spent the afternoon down by the sea, in full view of dozens of people, so she couldn't have done anything herself, and her old man spent the day in Naples, like Cesare and me, so he couldn't have done anything, either. But that doesn't mean they haven't a hand in it somehow. If you want to know what I think ..."

"Well?"

"I think you've been picked on simply because you're the one person in our lot who hasn't got any alibi to speak of. I don't suppose they've anything against you personally, but you just happen not to be able to prove too easily where you were, so it's convenient to use you. They want you to be suspected so that certain things about them won't be looked into too closely. It may be, for instance, that Mr. Ranzi's alibi won't stand up to too much inspection. Maybe he didn't go to Naples at all."

"You didn't see him on the train you went by yourselves?"

"No, but that doesn't mean anything. We could have

missed him in the crowd, or he could have gone earlier or later."

"Madge, do you know for sure that Mr. Ballard went to Naples that morning?"

Madge sucked the last few drops of brandy out of her glass. "Interesting your asking that," she said. "Cesare and I don't agree about it, you see. Cesare says he did, but all I can say is, I saw him get on the train."

"You didn't travel with him, then?"

"Lord, no. We don't travel first class, Cesare and me."

"But Cesare saw him at Naples?"

"So he says."

"Don't you believe him?"

Madge gave another of her shrugs. "I've no reason not to, but I've got in the habit of never believing anything Cesare says that I haven't seen with my own eyes. My God, how that man can lie! I think he lies to amuse himself, because half the time it doesn't do him any good. D'you know what I caught him telling those policemen this morning?"

Ruth shook her head.

"He was saying . . ." Madge had a half-smile on her face when she started the sentence, as if there had been some humour about Cesare's lie. But as she paused, the smile disappeared and her face became sober and anxious. "It was about you, love, and I don't like to tell it you, yet it's really what I came in here to say and why I gave myself a drink first. There are some sorts of things I don't find easy to say, anyway not to a person's face, when I've got to admit it's my own husband who's spreading the story, the dirty little rat. Not that he's the only one who's been spreading it. I've heard it from others too and always told them what I thought of them. But there are some things that stick, particularly in the mind of an Italian policeman."

"What was it, what was it?" Ruth asked impatiently.

"That there was something between you and Mr. Ballard, love."

Ruth drew a deep breath. At hearing this story again, she felt a blind rage, which made her think that she had been a fool to drink the brandy. She could not afford blind rages now.

" That's really been said by a lot of people, has it ? "
she asked unsteadily.

" Well, what do you expect ? " Madge said. She stood up.
" An attractive girl like you and a man like him. But
Cesare knew there wasn't a word of truth in it. I could have
killed him when I heard it."

For a moment she waited, seeming to be expecting Ruth
to speak. But when Ruth said nothing, Madge added,
" There's some lunch ready for you when you want it, love.
We had ours while you were out. You don't want to forget
to eat, however worried you are. I'll put it out on the terrace
now, shall I ? "

" Thanks, Madge." Ruth ran the tip of her tongue along
her lips. " This story about me—if people really believe
it—it might give me a motive, mightn't it ? *Crime passionel*
—my God ! "

" That's why I had to tell you about it," Madge said.
" If those Ranzis are trying to put suspicion on you, this talk
there's been will help them to make trouble."

" But people can't really believe it," Ruth insisted. " I
never made much secret of the fact that I disliked Lester
intensely. He certainly knew that himself. In fact, now
that I come to think of it, I almost wonder if he didn't
arrange . . ."

She stopped herself in horror and only just in time. If
she had spoken a few more words, she would have given
away to Madge not only some of the facts concerning Lester
Ballard's intended disappearance, but far more besides.

Ruth put down her glass with a look of distaste. Certainly
the brandy had been a mistake. For what she had been
about to say was that she almost wondered whether Lester
himself had not planned, as a form of revenge for her dislike
of him and for her championing of Nicky against him, that
she should be suspected of the murder of the Lester Ballard
who was to be found dead in the ravine. A necessary part
of such a plan would have been the spreading of the story,
by Marguerite and himself, that Ruth was in love with him
and perhaps even his mistress, while Marguerite's invitation for the afternoon would have been a deliberate
trap, so that Ruth should find herself without any reliable
alibi.

Madge was saying, " When a woman makes a parade of her dislike for a man, love, nine people out of ten jump to the conclusion she's just putting up a smoke-screen to hide her real feelings, either from him, herself, or the neighbours. And nine times out of ten they're right, anyway when the man's good-looking enough and popular with other women and reasonably rich. You and me know that this happens to have been the tenth time—and so does Cesare, damn him ! But that doesn't mean we'll be able to stop the gossip."

From the doorway her husband's pleasant voice inquired, " Why are you damning poor Cesare ? "

He was standing there and how long he had been standing there neither of them could have told. In one hand he was holding a bunch of freshly-gathered pink geraniums.

Madge turned on him in fury.

" You know well enough what I'm damning you for, you creeping, snooping little devil ! You know what I think of your lies and your tale-spreading. You think you can get away with anything. But I'm warning you, you'd better be careful. You might go too far, even with me. There are things I could spread about you if I choose. . . . And what do you think you're doing with those flowers there ? We don't want any flowers."

He ignored the rest of what she had said and replied tranquilly to the last remark. " But they are so pretty. I picked them for the *signorina* because she looks so sad and worried."

" Miss Ruth doesn't like pink geraniums," Madge said, " and I don't want any flowers cluttering up my kitchen. You can take them away and get rid of them."

" The *signorina* doesn't like pink geraniums ? " Cesare repeated wonderingly.

" No," Madge said. " I put geraniums in the vase here yesterday and Miss Ruth changed them to oleanders. Now go away and don't bother us."

" But I came to tell you something," Cesare said apologetically. He looked regretfully at the bunch of flowers in his hand and softly caressed one of the blooms with the tips of his fingers. " The Signor Brigadiere from the *Questura* is here again and wishes to speak with the *signorina*."

He stepped aside and the detective who had come to the villa that morning with the other police officers came into the room.

Ruth did not even look at him. She could not remove her eyes from the bunch of pink geraniums and Cesare's dark, smiling face above them.

XIV

GREETING RUTH formally, Cirio stood glancing about the room with his indifferent and slightly irritable gaze until the Gargiulos had gone. Then, at Ruth's invitation, he sat down. His presence had an oddly soothing effect on her. After the shock that she had just had, she had a feeling that this man was really on her side. He had no mysterious or evil intentions concerning her. He was offering her neither friendship nor enmity, nor one disguised as the other. He merely wanted the truth. He made the world feel sane.

For Ruth this was a dangerous moment. If Cirio had known the right words to use just then, she might easily have told him everything she knew.

In fact he seemed not to know how to begin at all, but sat with a frown on his narrow face, looking at her inquiringly, as if he had already asked her a question and was giving her time to consider her answer.

At last he said, " You have been down into San Antioco this morning. ? "

" Yes," Ruth said.

" You saw Signora Ranzi there ? "

" Yes."

" And Signor Evers ? "

So Stephen had been right. They had been keeping an eye on her.

" Yes," she said.

" I have had to question them concerning the account you gave of your activities yesterday. You understand, that is necessary. I have to do it with everyone."

" Of course."

" Signor Evers corroborates what you said about the time that you spent in his company. Signora Ranzi does not."

" I know," Ruth said.

Cirio raised his thin, dark eyebrows. " You knew that she would not when you told us of your invitation from her ? "

" No, naturally I didn't know it then."

He waited a moment, then said, " Would you like to explain that ? "

" I wish I could," she said. " Unfortunately, I don't understand it myself. What I told you is true and what she told you is untrue. That's all I can say."

A little to her surprise, he did not reject this statement out of hand.

" Is there no one else who can corroborate any part of your story ? " he asked.

" It's possible that Nicky Ballard heard me speaking on the telephone to Signora Ranzi," Ruth said, " but I'm not actually sure of that. Perhaps he'd left the house already. I think he probably had. And even if he did hear me, he couldn't, of course, prove that it was Signora Ranzi to whom I was speaking."

" No, just so." He began tapping with his hand on his knee. The little nervous movement made Ruth think that his mind was engrossed with something other than the questions he was asking and that he hardly cared what replies she gave to them. " This boy, I have very different accounts of him from different people," he said.

" So I should have expected," she answered.

" I find his disappearance very mysterious. There seems to be no possibility that he could have been involved in his father's death, for the murderer unquestionably was able to drive a car and I find that everyone agrees that the boy was quite unable to do that. So his flight is puzzling, unless we suppose that he happened to witness the murder and believed himself to be in danger from the murderer on account of it. That is not impossible. Another possibility is that he did not go away of his own free will, in which case, we must consider that some harm may have befallen him."

" You're searching for him ? "

" Of course, in every way we can. But now, to return to the question of your movements yesterday." The finger was still tapping his knee. "Supposing that your story is correct and that Signora Ranzi's denial of it is false, what reason do you suggest for this strange behaviour of hers?"

His tone was so reasonable, so quietly impersonal, and his pale, rather tired face was so intelligent, whilst not being unkind, that it seemed impossible that there could be any danger in answering him honestly. It felt as if far the best thing to say was that Marguerite Ranzi had conspired with Lester Ballard to commit a murder, that it had been necessary for the carrying out of their plan that Ruth should be absent from the house for the afternoon when the murder was to be committed; that it had been impossible for Marguerite to be at home to meet Ruth at the appointed time because it had been necessary for Marguerite's car to be waiting where Lester Ballard could easily take it; that from spite or from anxiety to save their own skins, they had intended from the first that Ruth should come under suspicion; and finally, that she, Ruth, could prove most of this by showing the *brigadiere* two forged passports and two tickets to Buenos Aires. It would have been a wonderful relief to give that answer.

Ruth met his eyes deliberately and said, "I suppose she must dislike me more than I've ever realised."

"For no reason—an almost insane dislike?" Cirio asked.

"She may have a reason," Ruth replied. "I may have offended her in some way that I don't know about."

He gave a shake of his head.

"Well, I can't explain it any further," she said.

"That's a pity," he said, "because . . ."

"Yes?"

The frown had deepened on his narrow forehead.

"Think!" he said abruptly. "Think! Did no one see you go into that house or come out of it? Have you no proof of what you say?"

"There was a note," Ruth said. "Mrs. Ranzi left a note on the drawing-room table, asking me to wait for her. Before I left, I scribbled a few words on the same piece of paper, saying I'd waited as long as I could."

"Where is that note now?"

"Destroyed, I imagine."

"Yes, certainly, if what you say is true."

"It is true."

He stood up. "It may be, it may be. You understand, I do not say yet that it isn't. But we have to test everything. You are not the only one who cannot explain all your movements yesterday. Signor Evers, for instance, cannot prove how he spent the period between the time you left him and the time when he joined Signora Ranzi in the cove here. He says he was in his hotel, and perhaps he was, but no one else appears to have seen him. The two Gargiulos spent the day in Naples, Signora Gargiulo with her mother-in-law, her husband with various friends. Signor Ranzi also spent the day there in his office, where several people can vouch for him, and Signora Ranzi spent the whole afternoon in the cove. But these are not the only people with whom we may have to concern ourselves. It may be that the roots of this murder are not to be found in San Antioco at all."

Ruth had hardly listened to the last part of this speech. "Did you say that there's a period of time that Stephen Evers can't account for?" she said. "I thought that he went to the cove as soon as he and I separated."

"Oh, no, it was not until more than an hour later."

Without warning, Cirio suddenly walked across the room. He went to the green and white striped couch that stood under the window and taking hold of one arm, jerked the couch away from the wall. For an eternity he stood there, looking expressionlessly at the back of the couch. Then he pushed it back into it place. His dark, tired eyes looked into Ruth's.

"*Signorina*, find that note," he said.

Ruth could not have answered a word. She knew that her face had gone quite white.

Cirio went to the door. As he reached it, Ruth got to her feet and followed him out on to the terrace. Then she managed to speak.

"Signor Brigadiere, I meant to ask you, have you seen Signor Sebastiano yet?"

"Yes," he said, "in Naples, this morning."

"No, I mean since then, within this last half hour. He's just been here, you know."

"No, I didn't know that," he said.

".Perhaps he's waiting for you now at the *Commissariat*. He's got something very important to tell you."

" I see. I am going there now."

" Good-bye, then."

" Good-bye. And find that note—please find that note ! "

He went out to his waiting jeep.

The moment that he had gone Ruth turned and ran into the house. She ran to the couch and wrenched it away from the wall. It was very heavy and needed all her strength. Looking behind it, she saw what Cirio had seen. There were several stains there, showing dull brown against the striped fabric.

Outside a series of rockets exploded into the sky. They were nearer at hand than any that she had heard before. She wanted to cover her ears against them. She hated the sound of them.

Cirio's words had begun to repeat in her head. Find that note. Find that note. Find that note. . . .

No, that was useless, for the note certainly did not exist any more. A few ashes on the wind or down a drain was all that was left of it by now. There would not be so much of it left as one of the charred scraps of paper drifting down out of the sky after a rocket had exploded.

But perhaps there had been someone who had seen her go into the Ranzis' house or come out of it. If she thought hard. . . .

She heard herself laughing. Of course there had been someone. Of course, of course. The laughter welled in her. She ran to the telephone.

She gave the number of Stephen's hotel. When a voice answered, she asked for Stephen. She was told to wait. A minute or two later, Stephen spoke to her, " Ruth ? "

" The *carozza* driver," Ruth said, " Giulio. The one in the pork-pie hat."

There was a silence, then Stephen said, " Oh, yes ? "

" He saw me," Ruth went on excitedly. " He saw me leaving the Ranzis' house. He was coming down the hill as I came out. I've been a fool not to remember it before. Can you find him, Stephen ? Can you ask him if he remembers it all right ? "

" Giulio," Stephen said. " A pork-pie hat. I'll do my

best." He waited again for a moment. " Has something happened ? Your voice sounds strange."

"Oh, yes, a lot has happened," she said. " That detective's just been here. And Amedeo. . . . And Madge has been telling me things. . . . Stephen, I've *got* to be able to prove that I went to the Ranzi's house. I've simply got to. But it's all right, I can. Giulio saw me come out and he drove along beside me for a little way, trying to persuade me to let him drive me up here. Can you go and look for him, now ? "

" Yes, if he's around the place, I'll find him. But he may have taken some people off somewhere for the day, so don't count on immediate results."

" All right," she said, " but you'll let me know if you can find him or not, won't you ? "

" Yes, I'll do that. Ruth, I know you can't talk on the telephone, but something's happened to scare you badly, hasn't it ? "

" Well . . . yes. That *agente* from the *Questura*, he found. . . ."

" Don't go on. I'll go and look for your Giulio and then I'll come along and see you. You'll be there ? "

" Yes."

" And don't be frightened, Ruth. You mustn't be frightened."

He rang off.

Ruth put the telephone down and walked out on to the terrace. Madge had put some lunch on the table in the shade of the wistaria and the passiflora. There was a jug of water there, with ice-cubes rapidly dissolving in it. Ruth crossed to the table, poured out a glass of water and drank. Stephen had apparently been deceiving her about how he had spent the previous afternoon. Not that she could remember his saying in so many words that on leaving her he had gone straight to meet Marguerite in the cove. But certainly that was what he had let her believe. Still, for the moment, that seemed totally unimportant and what did seem of the greatest importance in the world was the unexpected protectiveness that had suddenly slipped into his voice.

Ruth ate most of the food that Madge had prepared for her, finding that she was much hungrier than she had realised and that the meal did her a surprising amount of good. But her sleepless night was telling on her and the afternoon heat weighed on her like a load. The breeze of the morning had died away and a shimmering haze quite veiled the far side of the bay. Only the cones of the mountain-tops floated high in the air. The sea was motionless.

She sat waiting, wondering how to pass the time till Stephen came. It did not seem possible to read and yet, if she did nothing, she was afraid that she might fall asleep there on the terrace. The air throbbed drowsily with the sound of the cicadas and the glare reflected from the white walls of the house made her want to close her eyes.

It had been at about this time yesterday that she had sat waiting in the Ranzis' house while murder was being done here. First one murder, then another. But it was all right now, she could prove where she had been. She had her alibi.

Some words went through her head. " Where hast thou been, sister ? " " Killing swine." That was the witches in Macbeth, of course.

Did they think she was a witch then, that when they asked her where she had been, they could expect the answer, " Killing swine ? "

It was really incredibly stupid of them. If there was a witch involved in this case, it was not herself. If there was one who could do black magic, who could deceive men's eyes, floating invisibly through the air to do her deed of darkness while her body, perhaps, lay stretched on the sun-baked rocks by the blue sea, it was not Ruth Seabright. Only now, she told herself sleepily, it was she who was being stupid, for witches had gone out of circulation a long time before and being in two places at the same time was no longer, in law, considered possible.

Perhaps Ruth would have fallen asleep at about that point if she had not happened to hear, from far down the road, the *clop, clop* of a horse's hoofs.

She got up and walked to the railing above the road. Round the bend in the road came a *carozza*, driven by Giulio, with Stephen riding in it as a passenger. Stephen waved to her and, Giulio, on seeing her, took off his ancient green pork-pie hat and saluted her with a flourish. He pulled his horse up by the gate and Ruth ran down the steps to the road to meet him.

Stephen got out of the carriage.

" Well, I brought him," he said. " How much, Giulio ? "

" Five hundred *lire*," Giulio replied.

" Robbery ! " Stephen said.

" It is the tariff," Giulio said virtuously.

" There is no tariff," Stephen said.

" Well, then, how much you want to give ? You got the money, not me," the beak-nosed, piratical-looking old man replied amiably.

Ruth interrupted, " Giulio, you remember seeing me yesterday afternoon, don't you ? "

" Sure," Giulio said, " I see you, I remember."

" Where did you see me ? "

" Where ? " He thought. " In San Antioco, maybe. Or in Ravento, maybe. I was in Ravento yesterday morning. Very interesting ruin there. You like to go ? I take you very cheap, eh ? "

" Don't you remember where in San Antioco ? "

" Sure, sure," he said, " I remember."

" Where was it, then ? " Ruth's heart had begun to pound uncomfortably.

He gave her a good-natured smile. " Where you want me to say I see you, *signorina* ? "

" Then you mean you don't remember ? "

" Yes, yes, I remember," he protested.

" Didn't you see me coming out of Signor Ranzi's villa ? " There was now a note of desperation in her voice.

" Sure, sure," he said.

" Do you remember it or don't you ? " she asked.

" I remember—I see you coming out of Signor Ranzi's villa." He made it sound as if he were repeating a lesson.

She went on hurriedly, " And what time was it, Giuilo ? "

" Ah, the time—it was in the afternoon," he answered readily.

" But for God's sake, *when* in the afternoon ? "

" Two o'clock."

" No, no."

He shrugged again. " Two o'clock, three o'clock, four o'clock. What time you want it, *signorina* ? "

Hopelessly Ruth turned to Stephen. He grinned reassuringly.

" A broken reed, I'm afraid," he said, " but don't let it worry you too much. Here, Giulio, here's your five hundred. I'm sure you mean well."

" Sure, sure," Giulio said, making another courtly flourish with the old hat. " Two o'clock, three o'clock, four o'clock . . . I remember you. I always remember you very well. And I say it how you like, *signorina*."

XV

RUTH AND STEPHEN went on to the terrace and sat down. Stephen produced cigarettes and for a wonder had matches with which to light them.

" Now," he said, in a low voice, after a glance towards the house, " tell me what happened."

" There's some blood on the back of that couch you pulled across the room while I was talking to the police at the door," Ruth said. " The *brigadiere* found it."

" God Almighty ! " Stephen's face went pale. His eyelids contracted as he stared at her. " How did he find it ? "

" He went straight there and looked."

" Then someone must have told him something."

She shook her head. " No—that's to say, I think it was only the *maresciallo*. I think he realised the couch had been moved and mentioned it to Cirio."

" And Cirio did some thinking." Stephen pressed his fists against his temples. His voice dropped to the merest whisper. " But just what *is* he thinking ? That's the point. Let's work it out. He thinks that Ballard was killed in that room, but he can't think that his body was behind the couch when the police came, because the police had already found Ballard's in the ravine. Come to think of it, Cirio can't be a lot further on than he was before, because he must always have suspected that the murder was done here. Whew ! " He rubbed a hand across his forehead. " I don't believe the situation's actually as awful as I thought for a moment. I should take that agonised look off your face."

" You looked pretty agonised yourself," Ruth said.

" Do you wonder, having a thing like that suddenly shot at me ? Well, what else happened ? "

Ruth told him about Ranzi. This seemed more important to her than the visit of Sebastiano, but Stephen did not seem to think it very important, and when she described the old man's visit, he became extremely excited.

" But this is really something, this is getting somewhere ! " he exclaimed. " It explains a lot of things."

" I don't really see it," Ruth said, " except that now we know for certain that Lester was a crook, whereas before it was only a feeling we had about him."

" I wish I knew how to find out what ships have docked in Naples recently," Stephen went on, " and whether there was one from Buenos Aires which happens to have lost one member of her crew, a man who came ashore wearing a checked shirt and blue cotton trousers."

" Why ? " Ruth said.

He did not answer her. " There must be some sort of harbour register, I suppose, but I don't know anything about how those things are managed. Do you ? "

" No," Ruth said. " But how have you arrived at that ? "

" Listen," he said, " Lester was bolting to Buenos Aires, wasn't he ? And we were asking ourselves this morning, what was he going to use for money ? Well, now we know. Recently he'd been buying up stolen jewels, hadn't he ? But d'you think those jewels are going to be found in the safe in the shop in Naples ? Or d'you think he'd risk trying to get through the customs with any quantity of them in his luggage ? No, someone's been smuggling them out of the country for him for some time, taking a few at a time and depositing them somewhere in Buenos Aires. And then, when this man had finished that job for Ballard, Ballard killed him, because, of course, it would be a nuisance to have anyone around in South America who knew so much and who'd want a share of the loot. I think it all fits."

" And the number in the red note-book ? "

" If it's anything, it's something to do with the jewels and where they've been put—B.A. for Buenos Aires and the rest of it perhaps a telephone number."

" Are you sure you still remember the number ? "

" Oh, yes. But now tell me about Signor Sebastiano. He left you to go to the police, did he ? "

" So he said."

" Are you doubtful about it ? D'you think he was going to lose his nerve ? "

" I don't think so, no."

" And then what was he going to do ? "

" Go home, I suppose, or back to the shop."

" In Naples ? "

" Yes."

Stephen appeared to think this over. Ruth thought, however, that his mind was already made up about something else and that this pause was only like the pause of a diver at the end of a spring-board, a pause for the sake of balance, not a hesitation. Suddenly he stood up and said briskly, " All right, then off we go. I wonder if by any chance that old ruffian's still around. With luck, he may be. Wait a minute, while I go and see."

" But where are we going ? "

" To Naples."

" But will they let us ? " She hurried after him as he went down the steps to the road. " Don't you think the police will turn us back if they see us making for the station ? "

" We aren't going by the station." Stephen was hurrying down the road. Ruth trotted after him. " Look, that's luck," he said. " There's Giulio, having a nap. I thought that idea might have occurred to him. Now the whole thing's easy."

He went up to Giulio, who had pulled up his *carozza* at the corner where the path branched off the road towards the cliffs. Having got into the passengers' seat himself, he had tilted his green hat over his nose, folded his arms and gone to sleep. Stephen took him by the shoulder and shook him.

Ruth, in her turn, tugged at Stephen's sleeve.

" We can't go to Naples by *carozza*," she said. " It'll take us till midnight."

Stephen took no notice. " Hey, Giulio, how much d'you want to drive us to Ravento ? "

Giulio sat up with a start and again flourished his hat. " When you want to go ? To-morrow ? " he asked.

" Now," Stephen said.

" Now ? Why you want to go now ? " Giulio said.

" Much better to go in the morning. Much better to start early, see the view, see the ruins, have good lunch—I show you good place to have lunch, very good, very cheap—you go anywhere else, they rob you, but I take you to my friends, who give you very good, very cheap lunch—then maybe we go farther, hey ? Maybe we go to Pompeii. Not very far from Ravento and very interesting, very historical. You see everything, make pictures maybe, drink coffee. I wait for you. Then I drive you back to San Antioco in the evening. Big moon now, very beautiful drive in the evening, very romantic. We go to-morrow, hey ? "

" We want to go now," Stephen said. " We want to go by the mountain road and we only want to go to Ravento and we aren't coming back, at least not by *carozza*. How much ? "

" Listen," Giulio said with an air of intimate friendship, " I take you very cheap to-morrow. Much better to start in the morning. I say you everything on the way, all the interesting, historical things, you make pictures, we get to Ravento, you see the ruins——"

" Now," Stephen said.

" Now," Giulio said with a sigh, giving in to the realities of the situation.

" How much ? "

" You want me to take you to Ravento now and wait for you while you see the ruins and have very cheap, good dinner and then drive you back in the evening ? "

" No. Just to Ravento. We aren't coming back by *carozza*. How much ? "

" I surprise you," Giulio said, more confidingly than ever. " Three thousand *lire*."

" You do surprise me," Stephen said. " Two thousand."

" Three thousand and I say you everything on the way, show you very good, cheap place to have dinner. Three thousand is very cheap."

" It's highway robbery." Stephen said. He turned to Ruth. " Could you handle this a bit better than me, d'you think ? "

" Offer two thousand five hundred and hope for the best," she said.

" But even that's robbery."

" Of course. But you have to be brought up to this sort of thing. I'm no good at it at all."

Eventually a compromise was reached of two thousand six hundred and Ruth and Stephen, both knowing that they had failed shamefully in Giulio's view by giving in so easily, climbed into the little carriage. Giulio, with a great deal of whip-cracking, which satisfied his own desire for noise and dramatic display and had no effect whatever on the bony old horse, turned the carriage about in the road and drove off towards the mountains.

" And now," Ruth said, as she and Stephen settled back against the gay, print-covered cushions on the hard seat of the *carozza*, " suppose you're so very kind as to explain to me why on earth we're going to Ravento ? Because I never heard of anyone who went there except to see the ruins."

" There's a bus service," Stephen said, " between Ravento and Naples."

" Oh." She gave a dubious smile. " I hope you're right."

" I am, I can remember seeing a notice about it somewhere."

" You don't by any chance remember exactly what the notice said ? "

" Not exactly."

" You see, a bus service may mean a bus that goes once a day, or even twice a day, or perhaps only once or twice a week. If we get to Ravento and find there isn't a bus till next Tuesday——"

" Then we'll just have to see the ruins and come home again with Giulio, though personally I can't think of anything that sounds pleasanter at the moment than staying in Ravento till next Tuesday."

" Except that the police would soon follow us there."

" Don't be so discouraging. One should allow one's nervous system a little time off, even in the midst of a murder."

She saw the sense of that, though as the *carozza* had just turned into the road that led up into the mountains, she did not think that her nerves would have much chance to rest for a little while to come. Soon they would be passing the spot where the body of the supposed Lester Ballard had been found and soon afterwards, the spot where what was really left of him lay. The road was haunted by twin ghosts, and even with the hot sun on it, with peasants working in the vineyards on the slopes above, and with the afternoon sky as clear as ever, the place felt shadowed and sinister.

Like Ruth, Stephen became silent as the *carozza* approached the small shrine in the rock opposite to which the body had been found, and she felt him grow tense on the seat beside her.

The shrine consisted of a small painted image of the Madonna, set in a natural cleft in the rock. A few bunches of flowers, rather faded, stood in old jam tins before the shrine. Some attempt had been made to make a little garden there. Some agaves had been planted in a bed at the roadside and some brilliantly blue convolvulus trailed over a short stretch of trellis.

On the other side of the road there was only a low wall and then a sheer precipice, overhanging the bed of a stream that was almost dry at this time of year. Passing the spot, Ruth kept her head turned away from the precipice, fastening her eyes on the little Madonna with her expressionless pink face, her golden crown and her blue cloak, for as long as she was able.

The drive to Ravento took about two hours. There was no possibility of hurrying Giulio's horse and though Giulio at intervals cracked his whip above the animal's thin flanks and gave a strange, groaning cry, "Aaah, aaah!" which sounded as if Giulio himself were in pain, no reaction was evoked in the horse. Giulio was talkative and at every possible point of interest, gave a little lecture, showing Ruth and Stephen the place where a bus had gone over the precipice, killing thirty people, and the place where the Madonna had appeared to a local saint, and the place where the rocks, jutting out from the mountainside high above the road, had the appearance of a mighty, heavy-jowled profile.

"You see him," Giulio said, pointing with his whip, "you see who he look like? He's always been up there, the old man, hundreds of years, maybe thousands of years, but we always say he look like somebody. Once we all say he look like Napoleoni. Then times change and we say he look like Garibaldi. And then we say he look like Mussolini. But now he look like Garibaldi again, ha, ha!"

The *carozza* jolted on. The road wound up into a barren region, where there was nothing but the mountain rock with a little scrub growing out of it and a few stunted pines. Yet even here, occasionally, the mountainside had been terraced into carefully cultivated vineyards. The grapes were not yet ripe, hanging from the vines in bullety green clusters.

Ravento was in a valley, a village much smaller than San Antioco, set amidst the usual olive groves and fields of Indian corn. Giulio refused to believe that Ruth and Stephen had not come there to see the ruins of the old monastery and wanted to drive them straight to the place, about a mile beyond the village, instead of to the square, where they would be able, they supposed, to find out whether or not there was a bus to Naples that day. When at last they had convinced Giulio that that was what they really wanted, he turned his horse sadly towards the square, saying, " And you no come back with me to-day ? "

" No, thank you, Giulio," Stephen said. " But you'll pick up someone else to take back instead of us."

" Sure, sure," Giulio agreed. " Yesterday I bring a Belgian couple to see the ruins. They come to stay two, three days in Ravento. I take back an American lady. But if you change your mind, I take you back very cheap." He succeeded in making it sound like an offer of his lifelong friendship.

Stephen repeated, " No thank you, Giulio."

" This American lady, I tell you about her," Giulio went on. " She wear big ear-rings, dark glasses for the sun, much red on her lips. She tell me she has been to Pompeii, very interesting, very historical place. But she is very angry. They no let her into the *Lupanar*, she say. They let in all the gentlemen, but she have to sit and wait outside. Very angry, this American lady. I say to her, ' I explain, *signora*. This *Lupanar*, this is whorehouse—whorehouse is for men.' But she is still very angry that they have made her wait outside."

" Being too much of a lady to make the obvious answer to that one," Stephen murmured. " Well, good-bye, Giulio, and thanks for the ride." He handed over the agreed sum and a bit extra.

Giulio's hat came off again in a sweeping gesture.

" Any time you want to go Pompeii or Amalfi or anywhere else, I take you very cheap," he promised. " You send for Giulio, I take you anywhere you want to go."

He drove off while Ruth and Stephen looked round them in the small *piazza*.

It was a quiet and almost empty square where nothing seemed to be happening, except that a man was walking slowly across it, carrying a great cluster of balloons, while two Franciscan monks were walking up the wide steps of the church to the tall, bronze doorway. A few children, playing in the shade of an ilex, noticed the man with the balloons and trailed wistfully after him. Ruth and Stephen, at the same time, saw a post at the side of the pavement with a framed time-table fastened to it. Hurrying across the square, they began to study the time-table.

" There ! " Stephen said in triumph after a moment. " Didn't I tell you so ? Assuming that I've understood correctly what this thing says, there'll be a bus to Naples in about an hour. There's one bus out from Naples in the morning and one bus back. Or do you make something different of it ? "

" No, that seems right," Ruth said.

" So we've comfortable time for a drink of some sort." He took her arm and steered her towards a café at the corner of the *piazza*.

At a table under a striped umbrella, they ordered beer. The thin, fizzy liquid was ice-cold.

" And now," Ruth said, " go on and explain the next bit. Why are we trying to get to Naples in such a hurry ? Are you going to look into the question of ships from Argentina ? "

" If I can," Stephen said. " But the main thing is to get hold of Signor Sebastiano. I want to ask him a lot of questions about the gang. He may have known more about them than he told you."

" You think it was a gang killing, then ? "

" Don't you ? "

An image of Nicky rose before her eyes. She answered, " I suppose so."

" We've got to hurry, though," Stephen went on, " because

sooner or later they're going to find the body of the real
Lester Ballard, and then they're going to be able to make
out an even more dangerous case against you than they've
got now."

"Perhaps they've found the body already and aren't
saying anything," she said.

He looked at her sharply. " D'you think that's so ? "

" No, I've no reason to think it. But that *brigadiere* might
easily know more than he was letting on. . . . Oh, look,
we're going to have music."

Three men, one of whom carried a guitar and one a violin,
had approached from across the square and had stopped
near them. The one with the guitar, an old man with a
scrap of white beard on a pointed chin and watering blue
eyes, began to pluck softly at the strings of his instrument.
The violinist joined in. Then the third man, who was
short and stout, with a red face and waving black hair,
threw back his head and in a ringing, overblown tenor,
started to sing *Santa Lucia*. . . .

" Sometimes I think they've got only one tune in this
part of the world," Stephen said, " or else one gets so dopey
with this one that all the others start to sound like it."

" But Stephen . . ." Ruth's attention had been drawn to
the musicians only for a moment. " I hope you don't think
I know where Signor Sebastiano lives. In fact, if he isn't at
the shop, I haven't the faintest idea where to find him."

Stephen put his hand into his pocket. " I've got Ballard's
address book here."

" The red note-book ! "

" Yes." He drew it out. In doing so, he also dragged out
of his pocket a piece of paper which fluttered unnoticed by
him to the ground. Muttering, " S for Sebastiano," he
started to turn the pages of the note-book.

Ruth stooped automatically to pick up the piece of paper.
It had been folded several times into a narrow strip and the
end of it had been burnt off. She was about to hand it back
to Stephen when her eye was caught by some handwriting
on the outer fold. She stared at it in utter disbelief.

The singing of the red-faced man seemed suddenly to
become unbearably loud. The plucking of the guitar strings
seemed to be happening inside her head. Her ears rang with

it as with stiff, unmanageable fingers she unfolded the piece of paper.

There was the message in Marguerite's handwriting, " Ever so sorry to have had to dash out. Back soon. Do wait. Marguerite."

Below was her own answer to the message, " Sorry, can't wait any longer."

XVI

IF RUTH had been able to think at all as she sat looking at the note in her hand, she would have folded it at once and slipped it into her bag.

Stephen was turning the pages of the little red book and taking no notice of her. She could easily have put the note away and gone on as if nothing had happened, continuing on this complicated journey to Naples, waiting to discover his real object in going. Then she could have gone to the police with the note and told them where she had found it. Stephen then would have found himself with a great deal of explaining to do. It would have been very interesting to hear those explanations.

But she was too stunned to do anything but stare at the piece of paper that meant so much to her. She went on staring at it until some impulse made her hold it out and say, " Stephen ! "

He grunted in answer, still studying a page in the little book.

" Stephen . . ." Her voice shook. " Will you please take a look at this ? "

He pocketed the book. " It's all right, his address is there," he said. Then he looked at the note. " What's this ? "

He reached to take it from her, but she jerked it away. " How did you get it ? " she asked.

He frowned at it absently, hardly concentrating on the question.

" Where did *I* get it ? " His eyes moved to meet hers. " I don't know. Where did you ? "

" It fell out of your pocket just now, when you took out the note-book."

" Well, what is it ? "

" Take a good look."

She held it nearer to him but did not let go her firm hold of it.

Reading the note a second time, Stephen seemed at last to become aware of the hostility in her attitude. His face became anxious.

" What is it ? " he repeated more sharply.

" It's Marguerite's note, the one that proves she was expecting me at her house that afternoon—and it fell out of your pocket."

" Oh, God ! " he muttered.

He thrust his fingers agitatedly through his unkempt fair hair and Ruth suddenly heard herself saying angrily, " In heaven's name, why won't you get your hair cut properly ? It looks horrible as it is ! "

" Yes," he said, " I know, I've been meaning to . . . But look, this note . . . Ruth, d'you believe I took it ? "

" How did it get into your pocket ? "

" I don't know. I often find queer things in my pockets. Are you really sure it fell out ? "

" It didn't fall out of the sky on to Ravento."

" And you think I've been keeping it. You think that Marguerite and I . . ."

" How did you get it ? Why didn't you tell me you had it ? What were you going to do with it ? "

" Stop—wait ! " He grabbed a handful of hair at the back of his head as if this might anchor him to things that he could understand. " I've got to think. This thing got into my pocket somehow, so I must have put it there. That's certain. But the point is, when ? "

" You mean you didn't know you had it ? Am I supposed to believe that ? " Ruth was scornful.

" I don't see why not. Nothing's credible or incredible by itself, it's always a case of knowing the people involved."

" Like the match-boxes. Is that it ? Sometimes you have none and sometimes several, but very seldom just one, like other people. You know, that sounded very convincing when you told me about it, but now I'm not sure that I believe it at all. Little aberations like that are so very convenient when you're faced with awkward questions."

" Match-boxes ! " Stephen pounced on that one word and paid no attention to the rest of what she said. " Bless you, you've put your finger right on it. That was it, of course. No matches." He smiled with a look of relief.

" I don't know what you're talking about ? " Ruth said.

" Would you let me hold that thing for a minute ? " He gestured at the note.

Ruth immediately moved it farther away from him.

" Look," he said earnestly, " I swear to you most solemnly that I won't tear it up, burn it, damage it in any way or fail to hand it back to you after about thirty seconds. After all, I don't see why you shouldn't trust me, because if I really made up my mind to get it anyhow, I think I could."

" In spite of our audience ? "

" Oh yes, they'd only produce some really romantic music as an accompaniment to the little scene. All the same, that isn't actually my idea of the best way to handle the situation and you can keep the thing to yourself if you insist, but there's something about it that I'd like to show you."

Hesitantly Ruth handed the paper to him. She thought that she was a fool to risk it, but certainly it was true that he could have recovered the note if he had made up his mind to it.

Stephen folded the paper into a narrow strip so that it looked the same as it had when it fell out of his pocket.

" There you are," he said. " Take it and stop looking so anxious. Now you can see what happened, can't you ? "

" No," Ruth said.

" I hadn't any matches." He said it as if he were explaining the matter to a child. " I picked this up and used it to light a cigarette. Then without thinking what I was doing, I stuck it into my pocket. That's all."

" But when, *when* ? " Ruth said wildly. " And where ? I left this note in Marguerite's drawing-room. When were you there ? "

Stephen coloured. He shifted uneasily on his chair, then

he drank some beer and Ruth found herself all of a sudden wishing intensely that she had never asked the question and might never hear the answer. It would have been far better to have slipped the note into her bag when she found it and said nothing about it.

"You tell me something," Stephen said defensively. "Why, from almost the first time we met, did you try to push me off on to Marguerite? Was it simply that you couldn't stand the sight of me, or was there anything else behind it ? "

Ruth felt bewildered. She showed it by a heavy frown. Stephen scowled back at her.

" That's what I had to find out, don't you understand ? " he almost shouted at her.

" I don't understand a word," she said.

" For God's sake . . . Look ! " He began energetically drawing some sort of a diagram on the tablecloth, yet plainly it was not what he actually wanted her to look at. " I did go to the Ranzis' house yesterday afternoon. All right, I did. I did. I feel a damn fool admitting it, but I did go there. First I went back to my room and thought I'd do some work, but then I got it into my head that I'd got to find out what was really happening and that the only thing to do was to go to the Ranzis' house and see. If you and Marguerite were both there, that would be all right, but if you weren't, then—damn it, then I'd know where I was. Isn't that plain enough ? "

Ruth shook her head. She was aware that the three musicians had started a new tune, which was familiar and yet strange, and it took her a moment to realise that it was simply the Italian words that gave it its strangeness. The tune was *Whispering*.

" It isn't plain at all," she said. " What did you think was happening ? You don't mean you'd already some suspicions about—about everything that's happened since ? "

" No," he said impatiently. " But I wanted to get clear in my own head why you always avoided me. The first week or two after we met, I thought you quite liked me and then all of a sudden, whenever I tried to see you, you pushed me off on to Marguerite. I didn't notice it at first, but then it got me madder and madder. If you couldn't put up with having me around, why couldn't you just say so, I wanted to know. But instead I was stuck again and again with that woman . . . Well, yesterday I lost my head about it a bit. I asked you to come to Ravento with me and you put me off by saying that you were going to have tea with Marguerite, when I knew perfectly well that Marguerite had gone swimming, because she'd rung me up and asked me to go with her. I was pretty wild about it all but I didn't say anything and I went off back to my room. Then suddenly I decided I wasn't going to stand that sort of thing any more and that I'd got to get to the bottom of things. If you just didn't like me, you could tell me so. But if by any chance you were avoiding me for some other reason—I mean, if it was simply something to do with Ballard, or even Nicky, or—well, I don't know what I thought it might be, but I kept on thinking there might be something that wasn't just dislike. My vanity, you'll probably tell me. Only it wasn't. I mean . . . Well, I don't know exactly what I mean, but anyway I went to the Ranzis' house to make absolutely sure you hadn't gone there, and as I expected, there wasn't a sign of you. So then I went to the cove, to see if by any remote chance you'd joined Marguerite there, but you hadn't and Marguerite said she hadn't been expecting you. So after that I went up to Ballard's villa, meaning to tell you how I felt and get it over . . . And then I didn't, of course."

" No," Ruth said in a low voice. " It—it would have been difficult, wouldn't it ? "

A silence came between them, while the three musicians went on with their rendering of *Whispering*, making something lusciously Neapolitan out of it.

" This note," Ruth said at last, twisting the folded strip of paper between her fingers, " proves that——"

" To hell with it ! " Stephen said furiously. " I didn't steal it or conspire with Marguerite to keep it from you and get you hanged for murder, or plan to work out some kind of blackmail with it, or mean to use it in any other foul scheme you can manage to suspect me of ! I must have picked it up in the Ranzis' drawing-room when I couldn't find a match to light a cigarette, and used it—yes, that's what I did ! I switched on the electric radiator for a moment and lit that bit of paper against the bars. Then I suppose I stuffed it into my pocket and forgot about it."

" I was going to say," Ruth said, looking hard at her glass of beer, " that this note proves I wasn't avoiding you at all. I did go to the Ranzis' house, and I only went there because I'd promised some days before that I would. I'd much sooner have gone to Ravento with you."

" There's no need to say that," Stephen said aloofly. " I shouldn't have said anything about it myself if you hadn't started waving that note at me, accusing me of trying to get you hanged for murder. Suspect me of the murder itself, if you like—I've suspected you quite a bit—but the other was going too far."

" Do be quiet for a minute," she said. " You do talk an awful lot, don't you ? I was trying to say——"

" Never mind. I'm sorry the thing came up at all. We needn't go on flogging the subject half the afternoon."

" Are you going to be quiet ? I'm trying to say that I haven't been avoiding you at all. But I thought you liked Marguerite's company much better than mine, so I—I did my best not to be difficult about it."

" It's all right, there's no need for you to explain anything. I wasn't trying to work on your sympathies." Stephen had become very stiff indeed. " I'm extremely sorry about the note. I understand how badly you need it and I assure you that if I'd had the faintest idea that it was in my pocket all the time——"

At that point Ruth jumped to her feet.

" The bus ! " she cried. " We'll have to run or we'll never get on to it ! "

But even running, it was plain already, would not secure them seats on the bus. While Stephen fumbled with money to pay for the beer and Ruth hunted for some in her bag to give to the musicians, the bus, which had just shot crazily into the square from a side street, was rapidly filling with a shouting, bawling crowd of human beings. All were armed with the deadliest of elbows which they seemed to enjoy using on each other with the greatest ruthlessness possible, while bulging paper parcels and bags of vegetables were joyfully employed as additional offensive weapons.

When Ruth and Stephen edged gingerly into the fringe of this crowd, the first seats in the bus had already been seized with cries of triumph and by the time that they managed to climb aboard themselves, there was nothing for them to do but stand wedged together close behind the driver, unable to reach any strap or bar to hold on to, but hoping that by being so tightly packed among the others who had failed to get seats, they would manage to keep their feet when the bus started.

In the peaceful *piazza* the three musicians had paused for a moment, then begun again on a different tune. It was *Santa Lucia*.

The bus started. The twisting of the road required an almost continuous pressure on the horn. It also required that Ruth should keep her eyes shut, for to have gone on looking steadily ahead at the death that seemed to be rushing to meet her from behind each blind corner, nonchalantly negotiated at frantic speed, would have been more than she could do.

The jolting of the bus threw her and Stephen against one another. Stephen's arm went round her and held her close to him. Suddenly both of them burst out laughing and at that moment, whether or not she had any good reason for it, Ruth believed everything that he had told her about the note, about the box of matches, about Marguerite.

In her ear Stephen shouted, " We'll probably get there alive. After all, he does this twice a day."

She shouted back, " And Italians are wonderful drivers."

" Wonderful," he bawled as the screech of the horn grew louder and louder and the bus, swinging round a great jutting wall of rock, came face to face with a lorry, loaded with tree-trunks. The bus seemed merely to execute a few dance steps round the lorry and proceeded on its way.

The perils of the journey were increasing, for the dusk was falling and the rock wall beside the road appeared sometimes to pounce out upon them and stand deliberately in their way. However, the last stage of the drive was along flat roads and through dusty suburbs and Ruth found it possible once more to consider the question of why Stephen had insisted on coming to Naples. It still looked to her a pointless thing to have done.

During the last part of the drive, Stephen had become abstracted and Ruth thought that he was more worried than he wanted her to see. When they got out of the bus, he looked around till he found a time-table and he studied this with concentration.

Ruth, bruised and exhausted, exclaimed, " You're not thinking of going back the same way, are you ? There are perfectly good electric trains, in case you've forgotten that."

" No, I hadn't. But going by train may lead to questions. Still, there's no bus back to Ravento till to-morrow morning."

" The Lord be praised. Where do we go now ? "

" To Signor Sebastiano's flat. And I think we'll take a taxi."

" That's your best idea to-day. D'you know what I was saying to myself all the way down that road, Stephen, trying to keep my self-control ? , I was saying things about death being a necessary end that comes when it will come."

" Very highbrow," Stephen said. " I was saying—well, some of the things one says to oneself when one's in love. Some of them quite highbrow too, come to think of it."

" Obviously you're much braver than I am," Ruth said. " I had to try to persuade myself that I was ready to die before I could think of anything at all."

" I'm not brave, I'm very frightened," Stephen said. " As a matter of fact, just at this moment . . ."

" Yes ? "

" I don't know," he said. " I'm getting premonitions or something and I don't like them. D'you know what I'd give anything for just now ? "

" What ? "

" To be comfortably back in a laboratory, doing something nice and peaceful like a bit of glass-blowing. However, let's look for that taxi."

They found a taxi and Stephen gave the driver the address that he had found in the red note-book. Both Ruth and Stephen became silent now, and Ruth, feeling Stephen's apprehensions without knowing what was causing them, thought how safe and carefree they had been in the bus from Ravento.

Sebastiano's flat was in a tall block in a shabby district. Though the block itself had the remnants of gentility, some narrow streets nearby were noisy and dirty slums, full of strange smells and decorated with the customary bunting of washing, strung from house to house. Ruth and Stephen climbed a long staircase. It went round and round a narrow well, with two doors opening off each landing. Behind one of these doors they heard the raised voices of a violent quarrel, behind another a baby screaming, behind several the same music, usually too loud, churned out by several wireless sets. The place was neither quite dirty nor quite clean.

At last they reached Sebastiano's door.

" Does he live here alone or is he married ? " Stephen asked.

" D'you know, I don't know," Ruth said. " I know hardly anything about him. But how awful for him to have to live here with these stairs. They must have been killing him."

Stephen rang the bell.

" You'll have to do the explaining, as he doesn't know me," he said.

They heard steps inside the flat and voices. The door was opened.

" Ah, so you have come," Cirio said, looking out at them without surprise. " That is good. I hoped I should not have to waste time sending men to search for you. Come in."

He stood aside so that they could enter, then closed the door behind them.

They stood close together in the tiny hall.

Ruth said, " Then Signor Sebastiano did come to tell you what he knew."

" No, *signorina*," Cirio said, " he told me nothing. Signor Sebastiano never reached the *Commissariat*. He was found shot through the head this afternoon in one of the streets of San Antioco."

XVII

THE AIR in the little hall was stifling. It was difficult to breathe.

" In one of the streets?" Stephen said.

" Yes, and no one heard it, no one saw it. Does that surprise you ? " Cirio led them into a room in which another man was going rapidly and methodically through drawers and cupboards. " To-day there was a *fiesta* and there was a great deal of noise all the time. That made it very easy for the murderer. But I have been wanting very badly to speak to you again, *signorina*, since you told me that Sebastiano had been in San Antioco and had something of importance to tell the police."

Ruth nodded. She was looking round the room. The heat in it was almost unbearable.

Cirio went on, " Signor Ranzi said he found Sebastiano with you when he called at the villa and that he drove him down to the railway station, leaving him at the entrance. Half an hour later his body was found in a side street. He had said nothing to Signor Ranzi about not intending to take the next train back to Naples, in fact he had appeared to be in a hurry to catch it. But you had said that Sebastiano was going to the *Commissariat.*"

" Yes, he was. He didn't want to catch the train," Ruth said. " If he seemed to, that was only to get rid of Signor Ranzi. I should think that when he was shot, he was on his way to see you."

She sat down exhaustedly. It seemed to her that she could not remember a time when she had not felt exhausted. Swaying against Stephen in the bus in the mountains and being caught in his arms and laughing together had happened in another life.

Stephen remained standing near the door. He was looking at her hard, wanting, she felt sure, to convey some message to her, but she had no idea what it was.

She started to tell Cirio everything, as far as she could remember it, that Sebastiano had told her. While she was speaking her glance roamed round the room. She was thinking that the price the old man had been paid for his silence about his employer's affairs had not been high. Though there were a few beautiful pieces of furniture in the room, which Sebastiano, with his knowledge of the subject, would have acquired cheaply, his poverty was obvious. There were only two rooms in the flat, one opening out of the other. Both of them had blotched walls and long cracks in the ceilings.

Cirio listened intently. But as she proceeded, Ruth began to have the feeling that what she said was not new to him and that he was more interested in the way that she was telling the story, in what she said and what she left out, than in what she had to tell. This gave her the idea that he had set some trap for her and was waiting for her to walk into it. But when she faltered and became muddled about some of the things that the old man had said, Cirio only waited for her to continue.

As soon as she stopped, Stephen, still standing by the door, said to Cirio, " You knew most of this, didn't you? "

So Stephen had had the same impression as she, concerning the *agente*.

Cirio replied, " It is true that if he had not been killed, Signor Ballard's activities would not have continued much longer."

" Did he know that? " Stephen asked.

" Possibly," Cirio said. " Why do you ask? "

" I wondered, that's all," Stephen said. " I wondered if . . . well, if this gang that's supposed to exist knew that you'd got on to Ballard, that might explain why they thought of putting him out of the way. I imagine you don't know yet who's in this gang."

Cirio shrugged. " Perhaps we know plenty."

" And perhaps you don't," Stephen said. " If you knew all you wanted, you'd no reason for allowing Ballard to stay around loose."

" Except that one requires evidence as well as knowledge. And it is by no means certain that this was a gang murder. Signorina Seabright is not convinced that it was. In spite of Sebastiano's story, she still has her doubts. There are things she has not yet told to you or me and among those are her reasons for not believing in Sebastiano's theory of the murder."

Ruth asked quickly, " Why do you think I don't believe in it ? "

" But you don't, is that not so ? "

" How should I know ? " she said. " I heard this story of gangs and stolen property and so on for the first time to-day. And I've had a good many other shocks. I don't know what to believe or not to believe."

" You don't believe in it," Cirio repeated. " But that is interesting, because the story is so probably true. I wish you would tell me why you don't believe in it."

" Why do you think I don't ? " she asked defensively.

" You have an expressive face," he said. " It may be easier than you know for others to guess when you mean what you say and when you don't."

She shook her head. " You're trying to make me tell you something, aren't you ? But I don't know what it is, so why don't you just ask me and be done with it ? "

" I can tell you something she hasn't told you," Stephen said. " She's found the note. The one that proves that Marguerite Ranzi was expecting her yesterday afternoon. Ask her to show it to you."

" Is this so ? " Cirio asked Ruth.

She took the note out of her bag and handed it to him. He studied it, then asked, " Where did you find it ? "

Stephen answered, " In my pocket. It's a simple story, Signor Brigadiere, yet I'm awfully afraid you aren't going to believe it. However, let me tell it."

He did so. He told the story not very differently from the way in which he had told it to Ruth, and in the middle of it, he smiled at her. Ruth felt her cheeks flush. Probably, she thought, this helped to make Stephen's explanation sound convincing.

At the end of it, Cirio said cautiously, " It is a pity that this note did not appear sooner."

" It might quite easily never have appeared at all," Stephen said.

" Yet it appears just when it is most needed."

" If you're suggesting forgery——"

" I had not gone so far as to suggest anything."

" I know, you were just thinking aloud," Stephen said, " and I thought a little faster than you did. That's an unfortunate habit I've got, from which very little good ever seems to come. But the note isn't a forgery and my story of how it got into my pocket is true."

" Even that is possible." Cirio turned back to Ruth. " Are you sure that you have nothing more to tell me now about these three murders ? "

" *Three ?* "

" Two," he corrected himself, folding the note and putting it away in a wallet. " I apologise. I should certainly not have said three. But I am very troubled about the boy Nicky. I have the feeling that some ill has befallen him and the fear that was in my thoughts slipped into my words. I am very sorry, very sorry indeed, that I gave you that shock."

Ruth's heart was beating wildly. She tried to look as if she accepted Cirio's explanation, but she did not accept it. She believed that he had given her that shock most intentionally, and that the third murder, to which he had referred, was certainly not Nicky's. But how did he know ? How did he know that there had been two murders of Lester Ballard ? Had the second body, the real body, been found ? Had the person whom Stephen believed to have been in the house, watching while he and she discussed what to do with the corpse of Lester Ballard, been to the police with his story ?

But at least she knew now what Cirio had been trying to make her tell him. He wanted to make her admit that the dead man she had seen in the morgue had not been Lester Ballard.

Yet if that were so, she thought, then Cirio could not really know much about it yet, or he would have accused her, not tried to shock her into an involuntary admission.

Beginning to feel a little calmer, she at last risked a glance at Stephen. He was leaning against a book-case by the door and looking at Cirio with a puzzled, but not too puzzled stare. At that moment Ruth remembered a phrase that Marguerite had used to describe him. " One of those vague, rather hopeless sort of people who turn out to be awfully warm-hearted and efficient in an emergency . . ." So even Marguerite could hit on the truth sometimes.

"Is there anything more we can do for you now, Signor Brigadiere?" Stephen asked. "If not, we should like to go on our way."

"If you have nothing more to tell me, there is nothing else you can do for me," Cirio replied rather bleakly. "But your way is straight back to San Antioco. You will not argue that point."

"I'd like to." Stephen said, "but I won't, if you insist on it." He held out his hand to Ruth.

Cirio added, "You had some reason, I suppose, for coming to Naples and it was not only to talk to Signor Sebastiano. However . . ." He shrugged and gestured towards the door.

Ruth and Stephen went out silently.

The door of the flat closed after them, but a moment latter it was opened again and the man who had been searching through the drawers and cupboards in the flat came out and followed them downstairs. In the street he signalled to a car that was drawn up near the entrance to the block of flats, and showing by a jerk of his head that Ruth and Stephen were to get into the car, told the driver to take them to the station. At the station the driver followed them while they bought their tickets, saw them on to the train and waited on the platform until it started.

"All kid gloves so far, but firm," Stephen said as he and Ruth settled down, facing one another, by a window. "I wonder when the real trouble will start?"

"Stephen, he knows, doesn't he? I mean when he said *three* . . ." She looked round anxiously, not wanting to say more than that in a place where they could be overheard.

"He knows something," Stephen said, "but not as much as he wanted you to think."

"That's what I thought. But still, if they've found—it——"

"Perhaps they haven't. It may be that they've found out something about the other one. I think that's more likely. And since you're the person who identified him wrongly, they think you may know what really happened to the real one and they had a shot at startling you into giving that away."

"And did I give it away with this so-called expressive face of mine?"

"No, you did very nicely."

"So did you. But this trip's been a lot of rather wasted effort, hasn't it?"

"No, my dear. Actually we've done what we came for and some other useful things besides."

"What did we come for, then?"

"Well, I'd say it was useful that we'd cleared up one or two misunderstandings between ourselves, wouldn't you?" He leant forward, taking her hands. "They *are* cleared up, aren't they? We do both mean the same things, don't we?"

"Oh, yes. But Stephen, there's something I'm going to tell you——"

He drew her hands towards him and kissed the tip of one of her fingers.

"It's a bad thing to talk about murder in a public vehicle," he said.

"I know. I won't. But I'm going to tell you this thing as soon as we're alone again. I ought to have told you straight away, when you walked in and found me with . . . Still, I didn't know anything about you then. But I'll have to tell you now."

"All right, I'll come up to the villa with you and you can tell me there," he said.

"Yes." As she said it, however, she began to regret it. For it had just dawned on her that a moment ago, when she had asked him why they had really gone to Naples, Stephen had evaded the question.

Perhaps that was not important. But perhaps it was. Perhaps she still did not know anything about him. Perhaps she still had no good reason to trust him. Perhaps, perhaps. . . .

At what point, she wondered, does one completely overcome one's distrust of a person? Does it take days, weeks, years?

At the station in San Antioco they took a *carozza*. But it was a long time before they reached the villa, for the *fiesta* had blocked the way through the *piazza* with a solid mass of people. Packed tightly together, they made no attempt to make room for the traffic that was trying to force its way through. Rockets were still exploding in the sky and a religious procession, carrying images and singing, was approaching the square. As a path was cleared for the procession, the rest of the square became even more densely packed.

The sound of the rockets, so horribly like shooting, and the pressure of the crowds swamped Ruth in a wave of claustrophobic terror. But at last the *carozza* managed to emerge into a quiet street and drove on faster. The melancholy chanting of children's voices followed them. Looking back, Ruth saw the images bobbing above the heads of the people.

The *carozza* driver talked to them about the shooting in San Antioco that afternoon. He had the story wrong, for he believed that Sebastiano had been an important man in the black market, and that he had been murdered by a competitor. Neither Ruth nor Stephen contradicted him. Ruth was thinking of what she had intended to tell Stephen when they arrived at the villa. She did not know now whether she would tell it to him or not and she was afraid of acting on impulse and immediately regretting it. She was afraid that even if she reached a decision now as to what she should tell him, she might easily, all of a sudden tell him less or more. In fact, that was so probable that there was hardly any point in trying to think the problem out in advance.

It might really be best, she thought, if it turned out that Stephen had forgotten that she had said that she had something to tell him when they reached the villa and so give her a little longer to think.

But he had not forgotten it. When they had climbed out of the *carozza* and it had wheeled round in the road and started back to San Antioco, Stephen caught her in his arms and held her hard against him.

" Listen," he said in her ear, " I don't want you to tell me anything. I don't want to hear it. It doesn't matter, now."

" But——"

" Don't," he said. " It's all over. Don't talk about it."

Incredulously, as his mouth found hers, Ruth realised that he believed that she had been intending to tell him something about her relations with Lester Ballard. He had not guessed that she had been meaning to trust him with the name of Ballard's murderer.

"Hallo, mister," a voice said close to them in the darkness, "tell your fortune. Tell the lady's fortune."

From the deep shadows beside the road a small figure moved towards them. As the light of the moon fell on him, they saw that it was the boy with the budgerigar.

"Tell your fortune," the boy repeated pleadingly. "Very good fortune. Very important fortune."

He put his hand into the cage and brought the bird out. He set it on the edge of the tray in front of the cage. The bird immediately picked up in its beak a little envelope. The boy took the envelope from the bird and held it out to Stephen.

Stephen laughed. "Oh, all right," he said and put a hand in his pocket for some money.

But as he did that, the boy said, "No, no," thrust the envelope into Stephen's other hand, turned and ran away into the darkness. Before he disappeared, he looked back once over his shoulder. In the moonlight, his face looked pale and terrified.

Stephen stood staring after him.

Ruth took the envelope out of his hand and opened it. But it was too dark there to read what was written on the slip of paper, so she went up the steps to the house and opened the door. In the light from the hall she read a few words, written in pencil in an immature, familiar scrawl.

"Do not be afraid. I will save you."

It was Nicky's handwriting.

XVIII

She showed the note to Stephen.

" It's from Nicky," she said.

Stephen read it, then started down the steps.

She ran after him. " Where are you going ? "

" After that boy. He must know where Nicky is."

" Yes—yes, that's right."

" I'm afraid he's gone, but I'll try to catch him."

" When will you come back ? "

" As soon as I can. Don't worry. Go to bed."

" Yes. All right." She stood on the steps until he had vanished into the darkness.

Then she looked at the note again. Folding it carefully, she put it into her bag. She had not the faintest understanding of the note's meaning. Nicky must have got some even crazier idea than usual into his head.

But she saw now that she ought not to have let Stephen go in search of the boy without knowing the truth of what she had seen here the afternoon before. She had let Stephen set out in search of a murderer without knowing that he was a murderer. It would be best now if he failed to find him. Most probably he would fail. In the darkness and in the crowds of the *fiesta*, the boy with the budgerigar would have disappeared like a drop of water in loose sand.

She went into the house. It was as quiet as if it were empty, but there was a light in the drawing-room. When she went to the door, she saw Marguerite Ranzi sitting on the couch, so motionless that she might have been asleep. But her eyes were open. They were fastened on the doorway with a look of feverish waiting in them. Yet she still did not move when she saw Ruth, except that her lips parted slightly.

Remaining in the doorway, Ruth asked, " What are you doing here ? "

A shudder passed through Marguerite and the look of frozen immobility dissolved.

" I've got to speak to you," she said.

" Have we anything to say to each other ? "

Marguerite struck the edge of the couch a blow with her hand.

." You've got to tell me where he is," she said. " You know, don't you ? "

" Where who is ? " Ruth came no farther into the room.

" Lester," Marguerite said. " Where is he ? "

" Didn't they find his body in the ravine ? "

Marguerite sprang to her feet. There was rage on her face. " You know that wasn't Lester as well as I do."

" Wasn't it ? "

" Don't try any pretences with me. You and I understand each other. Where is he ? Where did he go ? "

Ruth turned and closed the door. With some surprise at herself, she realised that she was sorry for Marguerite. For Marguerite was in love with Lester Ballard and she did not know that he really was dead. Having helped him cold-bloodedly to commit a murder, she now believed that she had been abandoned by him. That he was lost to her more completely still than that, she had still to learn.

Ruth came a few steps into the room.

" I can't help you, Marguerite," she said. " I can't tell you anything."

" You can, you can tell me where he's gone and you're going to, too." Marguerite took a step towards her. " You don't think I'd give him up to anyone else after what I did for him, do you ? I helped him plan everything, I got you out of the way for him, I left my car where he could take it——"

" For God's sake ! " Ruth could not help a nervous look round. " Think what you're saying. Suppose somebody heard that."

But Marguerite seemed to be past taking in the warning.

" I'm going mad, not knowing why he went like that," she said. " I can't bear it. I can't sit waiting any longer without knowing. Why didn't he take the car ? How did he get away without it ? Why did he want it left there if he didn't mean to use it ? Was it all some horrible trick on me to make a fool of me ? Why haven't I heard from him ? Go on, tell me ! "

" You could ask one other question," Ruth said, " which

is, why did he want me kept out of the way if I knew what
he was doing ? "

But in her present condition, the logic of that went over
Marguerite's head.

" Yes, why did he ? That's what I want to know," she
said venomously. " Why did he ? "

" But he didn't. I didn't know anything. Why do you
think I did ? " Ruth asked.

" Because you were in love with him."

" Did he say so ? "

" Yes. He used to laugh about it and say he couldn't
help it. Now I know that was a blind. You were the one
who was really in his confidence."

" It wasn't a blind, it was simply a lie," Ruth said. " He
knew I didn't like him and I suppose his vanity couldn't
stand that. Really, you know that's true, Marguerite. You
don't believe what you're saying."

" Where is he ? " Marguerite came closer until she stood
within a couple of feet of Ruth. " Can you look at me
straight and say you don't know where he is ? "

For an instant too long, Ruth hesitated, then she said,
" No, I don't know."

Marguerite smiled. She had not missed the hesitation.
Immediately afterwards her manner changed.

" Please, Ruth—please," she whispered pleadingly. " I
know you hate me and I know you've got reason to. I lied
about that invitation—it's true, I did. But I'll put that right
if only you'll help me now."

" I can't help you," Ruth said. " Perhaps I would if I
could—I'm not sure. But there isn't anything I can do for
you."

" Listen, I'll tell the police anything you like," Marguerite
went on. She might not have heard what Ruth had said. " I
really will. I'll tell them about inviting you and about the
note I left and everything. And you tell me the truth about
Lester—whatever it is. I promise you, whatever you tell
me, I'll tell the police everything you want."

" I don't think you'd keep that promise," Ruth said.
" And I can't tell you anything, except that . . . No, I can
only give you some advice and I don't suppose you'll take it,
so what's the use ? "

" What sort of advice ? " Marguerite asked quickly.

" Forget about Lester."

" Listen, Ruth, please listen . . ." Marguerite clasped her hands before her. " I didn't want to harm you by saying I hadn't invited you. I just said what Lester told me to say. I didn't understand at the time how dangerous it could be for you. I never thought anyone would find out that man had been murdered and that you could possibly be suspected."

" Stop it ! Stop it ! " The scene was suddenly more than Ruth could endure. " Please go now. We've got nothing to say to each other."

Marguerite's tone changed again abruptly. " But I know you know something," she said violently. " I knew it yesterday evening when I came to see you and you'd just come back from identifying that other man. I knew there was something wrong about your whole manner. I knew you were pretending all the things you ought to have been feeling."

" Perhaps because you were pretending yourself."

" Perhaps—but I'm not pretending now and you are ! "

This was so true that Ruth's guard was shaken. She checked herself in turning towards the door.

Marguerite went on, " There—you can't deny it. D'you know how I know? If you weren't hiding things that you're afraid to have known, you'd have been at that telephone minutes ago, telling the police what you've heard me confess. But you daren't do it. You're as frightened as I am of their discovering that that dead man they've got in their morgue isn't Lester."

" But I think they know that already."

At the words, the flush that had come into Marguerite's face faded so suddenly and left behind it a greyish colour so ghastly that Ruth half-expected her to collapse.

" You're lying," Marguerite managed to say after a moment, but her eyes were wild with fear.

Ruth shook her head.

" Oh, yes, you're lying," Marguerite repeated. " But at least you've admitted you knew that man wasn't Lester. Perhaps you didn't mean to, but that's what you've done. So now you needn't go on pretending to be so much better than me. We can come to an understanding. You tell me the truth about Lester and I'll tell the police the truth about that invitation yesterday. That'll give you the alibi you want so badly—you'll be safe then. I'll tell them about the note. I'll write a note and show it to them, if you like, saying it was the one I left behind for you."

"They've already got the note you left behind," Ruth said. "Stephen found it and gave it to them."

"No!"

The cry was such a betrayal of the promise that Marguerite had just made that Ruth could have laughed. Yet at the same time she was horrified at what she was doing to the other woman. To inflict so much fear and pain on anyone, whatever she had done, made Ruth so disgusted with herself that she was very near losing her head and telling Marguerite everything that she wanted to know.

"No," Marguerite repeated. "I don't believe you." But she said it hopelessly, hardly troubling to make the words sound as if she believed them herself.

"It's quite true," Ruth said.

"Then—then Amedeo will find out I was lying. And you'll tell him why I was lying and he'll believe you now. And Lester's gone . . . Amedeo'll never forgive me and Lester's gone." She choked on the last words.

"I think Amedeo knew all along that you were lying," Ruth said. "And I think he'll stand by you whatever you've done."

"Oh no, you don't know him," Marguerite said. "He'll never forgive the blow to his pride. And he's an awfully cruel man. He might even kill me. He has killed people, you know. During the war. He's told me about it. Other people don't know what he's like. I've always been terrified of him. That was why I fell in love with Lester. He was so different. But now Lester's gone and Amedeo will find out everything."

"But he knows already," Ruth insisted, wondering how much Marguerite really believed in this portrait of her husband.

Marguerite opened the door. "If he'd known, he'd have killed Lester," she said and went out.

The sound of her footsteps faded. A minute or two later

Ruth heard a car drive off. When she and Stephen had arrived from San Antioco, she had not noticed Marguerite's car near the house. It must have been standing by the roadside without its lights. Marguerite must deliberately have left it without its lights, so that Ruth should be without any warning that she was waiting for her.

Ruth now decided to go to bed. But instead she dropped into a chair. She felt too tired even to go upstairs. At least, she thought, her tiredness ought to mean that she would sleep. The important thing was not to start thinking again. Yet the mere silence seemed to set her thoughts free to start another futile chase after one another.

Three main statements kept recurring to her in succession. Lester Ballard killed the man in the checked shirt. Nicky Ballard had killed Lester Ballard. Somebody else, not Nicky, had killed Signor Sebastiano.

Somebody else killed Signor Sebastiano.

Who? For this was the person who was dangerous to Nicky, to herself, to Stephen.

Then it started again.

At the same time, so unconnected with this sombre sequence that it was like a tune being played softly in a different room, her thoughts of Stephen went on in her mind. She half resisted them, feeling that at such a time there must be something guilty in happiness. But gradually the happiness became so much stronger than her fears and doubts that they were almost drowned by it. Getting up, she went sleepily upstairs.

She was half-way up the staircase when Madge came out of the kitchen. As she emerged, she was covering a yawn with her hand. She was heavy-eyed and pale.

" You've been gone a long time," she said. " Where did you get to? "

" I've been to Naples," Ruth said.

" Well, it seems to have agreed with you. You've got a look about you I can't say I've ever noticed before. You had your dinner while you were out, I suppose."

" No, come to think of it, I didn't," Ruth said, " but it doesn't matter."

" Aren't you hungry, then? "

" I'm too tired to be hungry. Has anything happened while I've been gone ? "

" You've heard about that poor old Sebastiano ? "

" Yes."

" Anyway you and Mr. Evers must have been well out of the way when it happened. They can't come bothering you about that."

" Have they asked you questions about it ? "

" Questions ! " Madge yawned again. " I'm tired of their questions. And Cesare couldn't say where he was either, or didn't want to. I know where he was and if the fool only knew what was good for him, he'd have admitted it."

" Where was he ? " Ruth asked.

" With that woman of his in San Antioco, the one he pretends he thinks I don't know about. But I dare say he told the police all about it as soon as my back was turned. He's not one to risk his skin for nothing."

" Well, good-night, Madge."

" Good-night, love. Try to keep that look on your face. It suits you."

Ruth went on upstairs. She went into her room and switched on the light. She was thinking that she had never known till that day that she had an expressive face, one that apparently gave away all her feelings to anyone who saw it.

She went towards the dressing-table. She wanted to look into the mirror to see if she could recognise this look that Madge had said she had seen.

Half-way across the room she stopped dead.

On the dressing-table, directly in front of the mirror, was a vase of pink geraniums.

XIX

It was like a blow in the face.

It must have been Cesare who had put them there, meaning this as mockery and a threat. Ruth would have liked to hurl them, vase and all, out of the window. But that would have been to admit that the flowers had the power to frighten her.

But how did Cesare know what they meant to her ? She wondered if it could possibly be by an inspired guess. If Madge, in cleaning the room downstairs, had seen the blood on the back of the sofa and had told Cesare about it, and since also she had drawn his attention to the fact that a bunch of fresh geraniums had been removed and oleanders substituted for them, Cesare might have done some quiet thinking and arrived at certain conclusions. Should that be the truth, he must be using the flowers now, not as a means of demonstrating his knowledge to Ruth, but rather in an attempt to trap her into doing something that would confirm his suspicions.

So long as there was the faintest possibility that this explained his sinister use of the geraniums, it was of the greatest importance that Ruth should do nothing to let him see that they disturbed her. However, she had no faith that Cesare was only guessing. Somehow, she believed, he knew what had happened in the house the day before. That meant, if it was true that his own alibi was unassailable, that someone had told him what had happened here. Someone besides Nicky and herself had been in the house and had seen all that she and Stephen had done. Stephen had been right in insisting that this must have been so. Someone had seen it all and had told Cesare to keep frightening her with the pink geraniums.

The same person had been to Stephen's room and taken away the clothes that Lester Ballard had been wearing when he was killed, leaving instead the checked shirt and cotton trousers of the other man who had been murdered. This again had been intended as a warning and a threat.

The same person who had done these things must surely be the unknown head of the gang described by Sebastiano. This person must be the murderer of Signor Sebastiano.

But a simpler explanation than all that was that Cesare had found friends who had supplied him with a false alibi and had himself been in the house at the time of the murder. If he was a member of a gang, that should not have been difficult to arrange. She wondered how deeply the police had probed into this question and what they really believed about it. Perhaps they believed far less than they had allowed her to think. They had told Ruth, after all, that Cesare had not been under Madge's eye in Naples. Madge had spent the day with her mother-in-law, an invalid old woman whom Madge often visited and who adored her, while viciously despising her useless son. But Cesare, the *brigadiere* had said, had been out all day with various friends. Ruth wished that she could find out what Cirio really thought, but she did not see how she could set about it.

By now her sleepiness had gone again and when she got into bed, it was only to lie awake, staring upwards into the darkness, hearing the occasional *ping* of a mosquito and finding the heat of the night even more oppressive than usual.

She lay without any covering. She ached with tiredness but she was quite unable to empty her mind or relax her muscles. Outlined against the mirror, she could just see the shape of the geraniums.

Every little while her thoughts returned to Stephen and Nicky. Had Stephen found the boy yet? If so, what had Stephen discovered? And what had been Stephen's real aim in going to Naples, the aim which he had said had been achieved, although, so far as Ruth could see, he and she had done nothing but obtain a view of the inside of Sebastiano's flat?

It almost seemed as if Stephen had taken her purposely on a purposeless journey, for it had not been necessary for him to take her to Naples in order to tell her that he was in love with her. That could have been done quite as well in San Antioco.

Had the point of the journey then not been to reach Naples,

but to get away from San Antioco, to get Ruth away from San Antioco?

At once she tried to blot out that question. At some point, she thought, you have to make up your mind to trust a person. You can never know everything about anyone, but at some point you must stop wondering about such things as whether or not the person could have removed you from San Antioco in order to make sure that the two of you should have a cast-iron alibi for a murder that was about to happen. You simply make up your mind not to ask such questions. You decide that certain logical possibilities are not possibilities at all. You do not go on to remember that that person had certainly been alone in the house for some time the day before and could easily have been the person who had mysteriously searched her room.

Her heart was at it again. Its thumping seemed to be at the base of her throat. This is what they mean, she thought, by one's heart being in one's mouth. For as she lay there in the hot darkness, a new pattern of events had just become distinct to her, and the outlines of that pattern were horrible.

Suppose it had been Stephen who had searched her room. Suppose he had done so because he believed that she had something concealed there that he wanted. Suppose he had not found it, but suppose that somewhere else in the house he had found the clothes of the man whom Lester Ballard had murdered. Suppose he had never undressed the body of Lester Ballard, but had simply gone through the pockets, taking out the false passports, the tickets and the red note-book, which he had taken back to his hotel, together with the bloodstained clothing of the first murdered man. Suppose he had then showed her the bloodstained clothes to frighten her and told Cesare to be continually strewing pink geraniums in her way to frighten her further. Suppose he had shown her the red note-book because he believed that she could read for him the riddle of the number on the last page. Suppose it had been for the red note-book that he had searched her room.

But suddenly she saw the flaw in the argument. It was not a big flaw. Perhaps it was not even big enough to upset the whole argument, but at least it was something. For the first place where anyone would have searched for the red note-book would have been in the pockets of Lester Ballard. Stephen would have done that and found the book. So if he had searched her room, it had not been for that, and what else was there, of possible importance to him or to anyone but the very pettiest of thieves, that she might have been thought to possess?

Her thoughts clung to this little flaw in her logic as if it had been the most precious of jewels.

Jewels! Could that possibly be the answer?

But those jewels were hidden somewhere in South America, not in her bedroom, and the importance of the red note-book was that it contained a clue to where the jewels were hidden. Anyone who knew enough of the truth to want the red note-book would not be looking for diamonds and rubies amongst Ruth's dresses and blouses.

What *had* been the object of that search, then?

Puzzling over this question, but finding no sort of answer to it, Ruth fell asleep.

She did not sleep for long. It was only a little past the coming of daylight when she was abruptly awakened by a voice calling under her window, " Ruth! Are you there, Ruth?"

It was a man's voice. Still half-asleep, she thought that it was Stephen's. But when she ran to the window and leant out, it was Ranzi who was standing on the terrace beneath her. His face, upturned to her, was grey with exhaustion. He was in a state of great agitation.

" I beg you, come down and let me talk to you," he said. " It is about Marguerite."

" Has something happened to her?"

" I don't know. I don't know where she is. I beg you, come down."

Ruth withdrew from the window. A minute or two later, in her dressing-gown, she appeared at the door below. Ranzi was walking stiffly up and down the terrace, his hands clasped tightly behind him. When he saw her, he came hurrying towards her.

" I know I wakened you," he said. " I am sorry. I am very sorry. I called to you directly because I did not want to waken the whole household. Will you forgive me?"

Ruth walked out on to the terrace. The air felt fresh and cool after the airlessness of her bedroom.

"What happened?" she asked.

"I don't know, and I couldn't bear it any longer," Ranzi replied hoarsely. "I knew she came to see you last night and I thought you might know something. She did come, didn't she?"

"Yes." Ruth went towards the table. The blue of the bay, softened by the morning mists, refreshed her aching eyes. "Haven't you seen her since then?"

"No, she never came back."

"She didn't stay here long after I got in," Ruth said.

"Didn't she say where she was going?"

"I thought she was going home." Since Ranzi's visit the day before, Ruth felt uncertain of him and spoke guardedly.

He started walking up and down again.

"When she left, she told me that she would not be gone for more than an hour," he said. "She wouldn't let me come with her. I wanted to come, but she said she had some questions to ask you that you would never answer if I was there. I knew that wasn't the real reason she didn't want me. It was what she had to say herself that she didn't want me to hear. But I let her go and I waited. At first, when she didn't come back, I didn't worry. Then I thought of telephoning to you to ask if she were still with you. But then I thought that after what I had said to you yesterday, you would not be very well disposed towards me and might refuse to answer me. Besides that, I was afraid—afraid of other things. So I waited. But she never came home all night. I've been up all night waiting for her. I've been walking up and down like a madman, cursing her and crying for her. What's happened to her, Ruth? What's happened to her?"

"I don't know, Amedeo, I don't know at all." Ruth had sat down at the table. She leant her head on her hands. "What was it you were afraid of when you didn't telephone?"

"Never mind, never mind. I know I was a fool. There was nothing to be afraid of. But when one has become mad with anxiety, one's fears are also mad." He came to the table and faced her across it. "What happened when she was here? I beg you to tell me the truth about it."

" We talked," Ruth said.

" Yes, yes, I know you talked."

" That's all. And then she went away. I heard her drive off."

" Listen," Ranzi said, leaning closer to her, " I know you talked. I think I could even tell you what you said to each other. If you are afraid to tell me that you talked of her affair with Ballard, you need not go on being afraid. Perhaps you feel some loyalty to her, in spite of what she tried to do to you, or perhaps you do not want to hurt me by letting me know of it. But you need not mind hurting me. It is impossible to hurt me. I am past being hurt. And there is no reason on this earth why you should attempt to be loyal to Marguerite. She was ready to have you arrested for a murder which she——" He stopped and drew back from the table. He cleared his throat. " A murder which she knew you could have had nothing to do with."

Ruth frowned in a puzzled way. " You were going to say, a murder which she had committed herself. You were. But she couldn't have done it, you know. She spent the whole afternoon on the rocks by the sea. There were lots of people there to vouch for her."

" Who knows ? " he muttered. Turning away, he stared out over the bay. " Who knows what she could do ? "

" She couldn't have murdered Lester."

He drew a long breath. " No . . . I suppose not. But all the same . . . Ruth, do you hate me very much for what I said to you yesterday when I pretended to believe Marguerite instead of you ? "

" I don't hate you at all," she said. " I was angry with you but I couldn't hate you for loving your wife."

" I was so afraid for her," he said, " but it was an evil thing that I did."

" I told her you knew of her affair with Lester," Ruth said. " I knew you did, after what you said to me. But she wouldn't believe me. She said you'd have killed him if you'd known."

" So I should have, sooner or later. If he were alive now, I should kill him."

" Marguerite thinks he is alive."

He whirled on her. His hollow eyes blazed. " What do you mean by that ? "

" That was what she came to talk to me about," Ruth said.
" For some reason, she wouldn't believe that that man they
found in the ravine was really Lester. She insisted that he
was still alive and that I must know what had happened to
him."

" Is this really true ? " He looked astounded.

" It isn't true that he's alive," Ruth said. " He's dead."

" You saw him yourself, didn't you ? You identified
him ? "

" Yes."

" Yet Marguerite thinks he's alive. She thinks he's
deserted her. Then that's why she was looking like a
mad woman all yesterday. His death she could bear, but
to have been abandoned. . . . There is no possibility of a
mistake, is there, Ruth ? It couldn't be that that body you
saw was not really Ballard's ? After all, I don't suppose you
looked very carefully. That wouldn't have been expected
of you. Perhaps you were wrong and Lester really is alive
still. And perhaps that's where she's gone—to meet him ! "

"No, Amedeo," Ruth said clearly, "Lester's dead."

" Then where is she ? Why didn't she come home ? "

" I don't know."

" Did you frighten her ? Did you harm her ? "

" I think I frightened her. And she frightened me. But
we didn't attack each other, if that's what you mean, though
I won't swear we weren't quite near it at one point. Is that
what you were afraid to be told if you telephoned—that
there'd been another murder done ? "

He shrugged. " Perhaps. Yes. I knew that for some
reason Marguerite had become desperate and when she
started to lie about her invitation to you, I began to think . . .
But of course, she was on the rocks by the sea . . . But for
a time last night when she didn't come home, I began to
fear that one or other of you . . . Ruth, I know I am out of
my mind. I have been out of my mind for a long time,
believing that with patience Marguerite could be cured of
her infatuation. There is nothing like a mad hope to drive
one mad."

" There was nothing mad about it. It—it was only a
little too generous."

" And you don't know where she's gone ? "

" No, truly, Amedeo. If I knew, I'd tell you. She got into her car and drove away."

" What state was she in ? "

" She was—very upset."

He sat down at the table. " I don't know what to think. I don't know what to do. If there were any possibility that Lester was still alive, I should think . . . But you say that isn't possible. I believe you. You seem very sure. And you seem very sure that Marguerite could have had nothing to do with his death. I should never have thought of it myself, either, if it hadn't been for her strange behaviour yesterday. Apart from her denial of your story, she seemed—well, not grief-stricken, but desperate and afraid and angry. So I began to think that something must have happened between them, that perhaps he had grown tired of her and told her so, that she had taken her revenge upon him . . . Yes, yes, I know she was down on the rocks, but the actual killing might have been done for her by someone else, some infatuated fool, like Evers, perhaps, who thought that he would possess her when Ballard was out of the way."

Ruth stood up. " I'll get some coffee," she said. Unless she moved, she thought, Amedeo would go on and on. " You look very tired," she added. " Some coffee will do you good." She went quickly into the house.

Going to the kitchen, she put water to heat and coffee into the filter. When she had done that and was waiting for the water to come to the boil, it occurred to her to glance at her watch. It was nearly seven o'clcok. That meant that by now people would certainly be stirring in Stephen's hotel. If she telephoned, someone would answer.

She went to the telephone. A woman's voice answered her and Ruth asked her to fetch Stephen. The woman was unwilling to do it. She said that Signor Evers was most averse to early rising. But on Ruth's assurance that the matter was important, she went to get him.

In a minute or two she returned.

" I am very sorry, Signor Evers is not in his room," she said.

" He's gone out already ? " Ruth said in dismay.

" No, it appears that he never came in last night. His

bed has not been slept in. Shall I give him a message if he should come in presently ? "

" No, thank you, I'll ring again later." Ruth put the telephone down. She returned to the kitchen and poured the boiling water into the filter. Her hands felt very cold and her mouth had gone dry. But there was no reason to be afraid, she told herself. Stephen's search for Nicky had taken him farther afield than he had expected, that was all. Nothing had happened to him. Stephen could take care of himself. She was not afraid.

But when she picked up the tray to carry it out on to the terrace, she could hardly hold it.

Cesare, coming down the stairs, collarless, with his hair uncombed and no shoes on his feet, exclaimed in surprise, " You are up already, *signorina* ! Let me carry the tray."

He took it from her and followed her out on to the terrace.

Ranzi was still sitting at the table with his face half-hidden in his hands. He looked up at Ruth.

" I think I know what she has done," he said lifelessly. " She tried to do it once before. I stopped her. But that was why I bore so much from her. I was always afraid. That cheerfulness and good humour of hers, it meant so little. It was only on the surface. Underneath she had always a great terror that some day perhaps she might have to go without something she wanted. She was very defenceless."

Cesare had set the tray down and was pouring out the coffee for them.

" I apologise for my dress," he said cheerfully. " I had not expected to find anyone here so early. But in this heat it is difficult to sleep. I myself have not slept very well."

His voice was as tranquil as usual. Standing back a little from the table, he smiled at them both. Casually he put a hand into a pocket of his trousers. Casually, as if he did not know what he was doing, he brought it out again. In the hand he was holding the red note-book.

XX

HALF A CUPFUL of hot coffee spilled over Ruth's dressing-gown. Ranzi started up.

"What's the matter, Ruth?" He was not looking at the spilled coffee, but at her face.

Cesare said briskly, "I will fetch a cloth."

"No," Ruth said. Her voice was louder than she had intended. "It doesn't matter."

But Cesare was walking off to the house.

Ranzi was still looking anxiously into her face. "What was it? What made you look like that?"

"It's nothing," Ruth said. She reached for the coffee-pot and refilled her cup. "You ought to tell the police about Marguerite not coming home, oughtn't you?"

"If she has not returned when I get back, I will tell them at once." He sat down again and stirred some sugar into his coffee. "Tell me, did you notice just now what Cesare had in his hand?"

"What was that?" Ruth asked jerkily.

"A note-book," Ranzi said. "A small red one. The strange thing is . . . No, I may be wrong."

"What were you going to say?" she asked, staring hard into her coffee-cup.

"Just that I thought it was a book that belonged to Ballard. An address book."

"It may have been," Ruth said.

"In that case, what was Cesare doing with it?"

"He may have found it somewhere." She still did not dare to look up at Ranzi, in case she should find that his gaze was less casual than his words.

"Ballard usually had it on him," Ranzi said insistently.

"But it may not be the same book at all."

"It had the word, 'Addresses,' written on it in English. How could Cesare have got hold of such a thing?"

She began to feel wildly annoyed at his pertinacity. "I don't know. I don't know anything about it."

He regarded her in silence. Then he said, "I'm sorry

—I know it isn't important. But sometimes one's mind fastens foolishly on details." He drank some coffee. " I suppose you still have no word of Nicky ? "

" No."

" Marguerite and Nicky, both missing . . . Oh ! " He started up and went to the railing above the road. " Here are the police now. I thought that car sounded like theirs."

" They're early," Ruth said. She finished her coffee and stood up. " I'll go and get dressed. I won't be many minutes."

But before she reached the house, Cirio and two or three other men came up the steps on to the terrace. Ruth stood still where she was. Ranzi came to her side and waited, facing the group of policemen.

Cirio was looking even sallower and more irritable than usual this morning, and there was something else about him that was different from the day before. Ruth could not say what it was. But she felt it and was scared by it.

She felt that what was coming was important and that it would be very difficult for her. Somehow she knew that this man, as impersonally as ever, was now definitely her adversary and that he had dangerous weapons to use against her.

He greeted her quietly. Then he went on, " I have some more questions to ask you. They are of a serious nature and I might ask you to accompany me to the *Commissariat*. But if you prefer, we will speak here."

" Thank you," Ruth said. " I should certainly prefer to stay here."

" Do you wish me to leave ? " Ranzi asked.

" You may stay if you want to," Cirio answered.

But Ranzi's question had been addressed to Ruth and he repeated it to her.

" Please stay," she said. " And let us all sit down."

They took their places at the table.

Ruth offered Cirio some coffee. He shook his head. She poured out another cup for herself and lit a cigarette.

" Now what is it ? " she said.

He gave one of his long, melancholy looks at the bay before he said anything. Then he turned his head and looked suddenly into Ruth's face.

"Yesterday you gave me a note which you claimed to have been the one left for you in her house by Signora Ranzi," he said.

Ruth nodded.

"You still say it was the same note?"

"Certainly."

"You still say that on separating from Signor Evers, you went straight to the villa of Signor Ranzi and waited there for about an hour?"

"Yes."

"You do not wish to alter that statement in any way? You do not wish to say that that note was written later by Signora Ranzi, at your request, to protect you?"

Ranzi was about to speak, but was stopped by a quick look from Ruth.

"Have you seen Signora Ranzi?" she asked. "Is that what she told you?"

"Will you answer my question, please?" Cirio said.

"The note that I gave you was the note that I found in the Ranzis' house that afternoon," Ruth replied. "Signora Ranzi would never have written such a note to protect me."

"You are friends, are you not?"

"No, we are not."

Ranzi insisted on speaking. "Signor Brigadiere, I implore you to tell me, have you seen my wife since last night? She went out in the evening to pay a visit on Signorina Seabright and she never came back. I am nearly mad with anxiety."

"She came here?" Cirio said.

"Yes."

"And you have not seen her since?"

"No—but have you seen her?"

"I am afraid not," Cirio answered. "Now to continue." His eyes again bored into Ruth's. "If your story is true, it is surely strange that you were seen, during the period when you say you were in the house of Signor Ranzi, driving the car belonging to Mr. Ballard from the garage here in the direction of the mountain road and that you were seen to return and drive the car back into the garage."

It was so utterly unexpected that Ruth's bewilderment showed in every line of her face. It was so wide of the truth, so completely unlike anything that actually had happened, that for a moment she could hardly believe that she was expected to take the question seriously. She could not believe that there was any danger in it. All that she needed to do was to say that the allegation was nonsense. She would say that and she would be believed.

Yet her voice, when she spoke, came hoarsely. " But that simply isn't true."

" You were seen," Cirio said.

" But I couldn't have been seen. I wasn't there."

" A witness has come forward," Cirio said, " who says that she saw you at the time when you claim to have been in the house of Signor Ranzi, doing what I have just described."

" Who is she ? "

" The woman in charge of the shop at the corner where the path branches off to the cliffs. She said she was sitting in her doorway and saw you drive the car off and presently return."

" But it's impossible—quite, quite impossible."

Yet as she said it, the sense of danger came alive in her. Looking at the faces of all the men on the terrace, she saw in them only a terrifying detachment. Even Ranzi, it seemed to her, looked inhuman. And the real danger, she felt sure, had not yet been unmasked. Something lurked in the preposterous accusation that had just been made, that was not preposterous. What was it ? How could she discover it ?

A nervous pre-occupation showed in her face as she sat there. As if he felt that he must penetrate it, Cirio spoke more emphatically. " This woman knows you well by sight. She saw you only the same morning, in the same dress and with the same scarf on your head and the same sun-glasses, going down to the sea. She is ready to swear to it."

" I see." But she still had not seen what she wanted to see, the important thing that lurked behind the accusation.

Then, all at once, she saw it. If the old woman in the shop had seen someone take the car out of the garage and bring it back, she must also have been able to see Stephen do the same thing some time later. If she had still been sitting in her doorway, she almost certainly had seen him. Not only that, but she had almost certainly told this to the police already.

But had the old woman still been sitting in the doorway

in the later part of the afternoon? Ruth covered her eyes,
trying hard to visualise the little shop as it had been when
she had been driven past it in the police car. Had that bulky
figure still been planted in the doorway?

Cirio misunderstood the gesture. He thought that Ruth's
defences were breaking down, that she was crying. Trying to
make use of the moment, he spoke more gently, " Come, you
had better tell us what you know. Why did you do what you
did? "

Ruth was pressing her fingers against her eyes so that
strange patterns wheeled before them in the darkness. She
began to remember a group of women by the roadside. A
group of women with buckets and jugs, waiting for the water
cart to come up from San Antioco. A fat old woman with a
red handkerchief on her head, sitting in the midst of the
group. The old woman from the shop. But the police car
had not passed the water cart on the way down the hill.
Probably the water cart had been late, as it often was. The
women must have had to wait for some time by the roadside.
Then there would have been all the chattering and joking
round the cart while the driver filled the vessels that the
women had brought, then there would have been some more
talking before the women would have been able to make up
their minds to break up the party. So after all, the old
woman might not have seen Stephen take the car out of the
garage and bring it back.

With a sigh, Ruth looked up. Her eyes were dry and
bright.

" It wasn't me she saw," she said. " She saw someone
wearing my dress and my scarf and my sun-glasses."

" She says that she saw you close to, wearing that same
dress and scarf, earlier that day."

" A light blue dress and a red and white scarf? "

" Yes."

" You see, I changed when I came back from my bathe,"
Ruth said. " I put on a green dress and I didn't wear the
scarf or the sun-glasses."

" You're suggesting that someone else put on these things,
deliberately impersonating you."

" Of course. And at that distance, how could the old
woman tell the difference? The scarf covers one's hair,

the dark glasses disguise one's face. As a matter of fact, I
believe that even from much nearer than that shop, one
could deceive anyone who didn't know one very well, at any
rate if one used some unfamiliar make-up."

"That is true," Cirio conceded. "But who then wore
your clothes?"

She could have answered, "Lester Ballard wore them."
But she shrugged her shoulders. "If you remember, I
wasn't here at the time."

"You have still to prove that."

"What more proof do you want?"

After a slight hesitation, he said, "I still think there are
things you know that you haven't told me."

She nodded. "Yes, one thing, at least. It's something
I've only just realised, since you came here with this story
of what the old woman says she saw. You see, when I went
up to my room, the night following Signor Ballard's death,
I found, as I thought, that my room had been searched. I
couldn't understand it. I couldn't think of any reason why
anyone should want to go through my belongings, but I could
see that several of my things were not in the places where I
always left them. Now, of course, I can see that it wasn't a
search at all, but that someone had come and borrowed my
clothes and not put them back in the right places."

She was pleased with this explanation. That search had
seemed so meaningless that perhaps it had been important.

Cirio asked, "Didn't you mention this apparent search to
anyone?"

"No," she said.

"Why not?"

"I don't really know. It was late. I was very tired. And
Signor Ballard's death had been a great shock."

"Yet you did not know at that time that that death was
murder."

"Of course not."

"So the search must have seemed to you a very strange
thing to have happened."

"It did."

"Yet you mentioned it to nobody. Were you then already
suspicious that other strange things might have happened
in this house?"

Too late, she recognised the trap. So she tried to make it appear that she had noticed no trap at all. " I think I just wasn't capable of thinking," she said.

" In the ordinary way, wouldn't you have mentioned such a search—to the housekeeper, perhaps, or Signor Ballard himself ? Or have you no objection to other people rummaging through your belongings ? "

" Of course I have."

" Yet you said nothing to anyone." He edged his chair nearer to hers. " If you had known already that murder had been committed, I could understand that. Where there has been a murder, other strange things may be expected to happen. There may even be danger waiting for a person who goes around saying that her room has been searched. People keep silent about many things once there has been a murder."

" I knew about the murder next morning," she said. " I hadn't had much time to talk to anybody."

He leant towards her. " I suggest that there never was any search at all. I suggest that you never thought of such a thing until this minute, when you saw that it would support the story that it was someone else who wore your clothes and drove the car that had in it the dead body of Lester Ballard. I suggest that you were here and not at the Ranzis' villa when the murder was committed——"

" No ! "

A voice cried the word loudly from the gate.

Everyone on the terrace turned towards it.

" She was not here, she did not do it, she knew nothing about it," Nicky Ballard said, coming towards the group round the table. " I can prove that, because I was here. It was I who killed my father."

XXI

NICKY WAS tall and very slim and dark. There was hardly any of his father in his appearance, except perhaps in the delicacy of his features. Usually he slouched and managed to make ungainly a body that ought to have been graceful. To-day he was holding himself stiffly upright. There was a deliberate and defiant assumption of dignity in his walk. He was dressed just as Ruth had seen him last, except that there were no bloodstains on the shirt that he was wearing. Someone had washed them away for him. He was carrying something wrapped in a sheet of newspaper.

" So," Cirio said quietly, " you have come back then."

" I have come back to confess," Nicky said.

He did not look at Ruth, that was the strange part of it, and something kept her silent and warned her not to move. The sight of him made her want to cry, only if she did, that would be the end of him. It would shatter him at once and turn him back into the uncontrolled and frantic child for whose mind and spirit she had struggled for four years. But it was painful beyond words to look at him standing there, after her two days of desperate deceptions to protect him.

"Confess then," Cirio said. Infuriatingly, he sounded almost amused.

Ruth knew that it was one of the most dangerous tones to take with Nicky, who had lived on laughing sneers from his father. But Nicky showed no signs of recognising the tone. He laid on the table the object wrapped in newspaper.

Cirio pulled back the paper. The thing it hid was a heavy spanner, that seemed to be coated in a thick brown rust.

" That is what I killed him with," Nicky said.

" This is what someone was killed with," Cirio muttered. " Very well then, go on."

Ranzi started to his feet. " This is not proper, Signor Brigadiere. He is a child. He should not be questioned in this fashion."

" I want to speak," Nicky said.

He was still not looking at Ruth, but straight in front of him with a nervously intent stare. There was some meaning in the stare which Ruth felt that she ought to recognise. But she was too startled and afraid to be able to keep her mind on it.

" Go on," Cirio said. " Why did you kill your father ? "

" I hated him," Nicky said. " I had planned to kill him for a long time. I should have done it in any case sooner or later. Then two days ago we had a quarrel at breakfast." He was rattling it off so rapidly that it was clear that the speech had been rehearsed. " It was only the same sort of quarrel as usual, only this time Miss Seabright was drawn into it. He was very rude to her and she was very upset. I heard her talking about it on the telephone to Mrs. Ranzi. Miss Seabright said that she couldn't stand it any more, and that she was going back to England. I thought that that meant that I should never see her again. But I thought that if I killed my father and got his money, then I could go to England, too. So I decided to kill him that day. I got on my bicycle and went for a long ride while I thought out how I should do it."

" Instead of going to your tutor," Cirio said.

" Yes. After a time I came back and went to the garage and got the spanner from the car and went into the house. I found my father——"

" Wait a minute. How did you know he was coming home early that day ? "

" I didn't. I was surprised to see him. I'd meant to go up to my room to wait for him. But when I came in he must have heard me, because he came to the door of the drawing-room and I saw him. It was a shock, because I wasn't really ready to do anything yet. He looked queer, too. That brown suit that I'd never seen before and that tie with the sunset and palm trees on it——"

" *What kind of tie ?* " Cirio's half-indifferent air had gone. He sat up tensely.

" It was an awful tie," Nicky said. " And he always dressed very well, you know. But this tie was all in violent colours with a sunset and palm trees on it. It caught my eye at once."

" And a brown suit, you say ? "

Ruth was shivering. But now that the revelations had started, she could not stop them.

" Yes," Nicky said, " though I don't remember it as well as the tie."

" Very interesting," Cirio murmured.

Ranzi exploded, " But this is all nonsense! Ballard was wearing——"

Cirio stopped him with a furious gesture. " Go on," he said to Nicky.

Nicky swallowed. His thin, long fingers began to twist round each other.

" Well, he spoke to me. He—he said something about my not being at my tutor's. I followed him into the drawing-room. I hit him with the spanner. It was quite easy. I'm bigger than he is. All that I had to do was hit him a few times. He—he fell down and died. He didn't speak or anything."

Ranzi pounded with both fists on the table. " But this is lunatic nonsense! Lester Ballard died from a bullet through his head."

" I doubt it," Cirio said, " and if you continue these interruptions, Signor Ranzi, I shall have to take this boy to the *Commissariat* where I can question him without any more of them." He turned back to Nicky. " What did you do then ? "

" Well, when I saw he was dead," Nicky said, " I started thinking that I ought to get rid of the body, but I didn't know how to do it. I can't drive a car, you see. And before I'd made up my mind what to do I thought I heard somebody coming and I lost my head. I bolted out of the house and got on my bicycle and rode off as fast as I could. And that's all I can tell you, except that I read in a paper that my father's body had been found in the ravine and I don't know how it can have got there, unless someone was trying to save me by making it look like an accident. But I know you know it wasn't an accident and I thought someone else might get blamed for what I'd done. So I thought I'd better come back."

" Oh, Nicky ! " Ruth said.

Nicky still would not look at her and suddenly Ruth knew why he would not. She recognised the meaning of his fierce stare straight ahead of him at nobody. Nicky was lying.

But what lie had he told? To the best of her belief, he had told the precise truth about what had happened here. The murder of his father, as he had described it, had been just as she had imagined it, ever since she had seen the bloodstained Nicky rush from the house.

What Nicky appeared not to know was that the body found in the ravine was not that of his father. Was that the lie then that was making his gaze so evasive and so fixed? Did he know that there had been two murders? Had he been in the house longer than he had admitted? Had he seen the first murder? Or was the lie of a different nature?

Cirio had continued, " Where have you been all this time? "

" Hiding in the mountains," Nicky said.

" Alone? "

" Yes."

" How did you get food? "

" I had a little money with me. I went into a village and bought some."

" And newspapers, too? "

" Yes."

" And you read there the accounts of the discovery of your father's body? "

" Of course."

" You read them carefully? "

" Naturally."

" What did you make then of the fact that they stated that your father had been killed by a shot through the head and not by blows from a spanner? "

Nicky shifted his weight from one foot to the other. " I didn't understand it," he said. " But you never can trust newspapers, can you? They all tell lies, sometimes on purpose and sometimes because they're so stupid."

" Is that so? " Cirio smiled slightly. " But suppose it was not a lie that the man found in the ravine had been shot through the head? And suppose, when he was found, he was not wearing a brown suit and a tie with a sunset and palm trees on it, but a silk suit, such as your father usually wore. What would you say then? "

Nicky frowned uneasily. " I don't know."

" That is what happened—that is the truth," Cirio said.
" So tell me, don't you think it might mean that the man we
found in the ravine was not your father ? "

A look of bewilderment had come to Nicky's face and
with it a look of fear that had not been there till then. It
was the look that usually came when he had to cope with
something that he could not understand. He always had an
extreme fear of having to admit that he had failed to understand something.

So he was not lying about that, Ruth thought. He had
not known of the second murder.

" But I killed my father," Nicky said helplessly. " I tell
you, I know I killed my father."

" If you were to see the body of the man we found," Cirio
said, " do you think you could tell whether it was that of
your father or not ? "

Nicky's face went paler, but he replied, " Yes, I could
tell."

" Signorina Seabright saw it and said that it was your
father," Cirio said. " Myself I have never believed that it
was, and whether or not Signorina Seabright really believes
it, I am unable to say. The strange fact is, however, if it
is not your father, that your father's body has quite
disappeared."

" Signor Brigadiere," Ranzi broke in with determination,
" on what grounds have you thought that that man was not
Lester Ballard ? "

" On the grounds that his wrists were uniformly sunburnt,"
Cirio replied. " Yet he wore on one wrist a watch on a broad
gold bracelet. The watch was not new. Signorina Seabright
identified it. She also said that Signor Ballard did not care
for swimming. If he had spent much time in the sea,
naturally taking off his watch, it is possible that he might
also have lain in the sun without his watch, in which case
the whole of his wrist might have become sunburnt instead
of there being a paler mark under the watch. But she said
he was not fond of swimming." Cirio took hold of a chair
and thrust it towards Nicky. " Sit down, Signor Ballard,
and I will tell you what I think really happened."

Nicky did not seem to want to sit down. He rested his
hands on the back of the chair and appeared to be going

to remain in that position. But then he abruptly changed his mind and sat down.

" I think," Cirio said, addressing not only Nicky but everyone gathered round the table, " that Lester Ballard was aware that he was shortly going to be visited by the police. For some time we had had him under observation, knowing that he was connected with a gang of thieves. We knew that his shop in Naples was the headquarters of the gang. But we knew also that Lester Ballard was not the head of the gang. There was someone else who was directing him, someone who had so far gone quite unsuspected. It was that person whom we wanted, even more than we wanted Lester Ballard. So we waited. But I think that Lester Ballard knew that his time was running out and I think he decided to disappear, and to do this more safely, he decided to leave his own dead body behind. Somehow he found someone to fit the part and arranged to meet him here in the afternoon of the day before yesterday. Yes ? " He turned his head irritably at a sound behind him. " What is it ? "

It was Cesare who had come out on to the terrace.

" Pardon, Signor Brigadiere, but may I listen ? " he asked.

Cirio nodded. " Well, I believe that these two men met here as arranged, and that Lester Ballard killed the other by shooting him through the head, then dressed him up in his own clothes, himself putting on the brown suit and the tie that so offended his son. I think he then carried the body to the garage, by the path through the garden, and put the body into the car. Now I have just changed my opinion about what happened next. I came here this morning believing that it was Signorina Seabright who drove the car up the mountain road, created evidence of the accident there and threw the body of this unknown man into the ravine. The man was small and she is a strong young woman. It would not have been impossible for her to do it. I came here to ask her to tell me what she knew of the present whereabouts of the real Lester Ballard, since it seemed clear to me that she was his accomplice. But now I think that it was Lester Ballard who drove the car, having disguised himself in her dress and scarf and sun-glasses. Having got rid of the body, he drove home again, returned the car to the garage as usual, went back to the house, and was making his last preparations for his disappearance when his son walked in. In another few minutes Ballard would have been gone. I don't know how he intended to get away, for it was obvious that he couldn't use his own car. That had to look as if he had driven home in it from the station, put it into the garage and then gone his usual, favourite walk up the mountain road. He must have made some arrangement for getting away, but——"

"No, no! Wait! You've got it all wrong. Oh, what a fool I am!" Ruth jumped up excitedly. Her cheeks were flaming. She had just seen the flaw in Cirio's argument, the same flaw that there had been in Stephen's explanation of what had happened. "And I really thought you'd done the murder!" she cried to Nicky. "I knew you were lying, but I didn't realise it was about that. Of course, you couldn't have done it. The man's got it all wrong, and so had I. Only I ought to have seen it ages ago."

Hands pulled her back. Nicky had jumped to his feet. He was trembling violently.

"I did do it!" he shouted. "Don't listen to her. She's just trying to save me."

"He's trying to save me," Ruth said. "He thinks I did it. But I didn't do it either. I can tell you who did, though."

Somebody started to laugh. The laughter was shrill and hysterical. It was Ranzi.

"You can't, you can't," he cried, standing up, shaking with horrifying laughter. "You can't prove it. You can't prove anything at all. She was down by the sea all the time. She may have left her car where he could take it, but she never came up here herself. You can't ever prove she did it." He started to walk staggeringly towards the gate.

"Signor Ranzi, come back," Cirio said. "Will you explain what you have just said."

Ranzi did not stop until two men went after him and took him by the arms and pulled him back.

"I can explain," Ruth said. "He believes his wife killed Lester Ballard. But she didn't. She couldn't have. She spent the whole afternoon on the rocks by the sea."

"But you think you can tell me who did do the murder?" Cirio said with irony.

"Yes," Ruth said, "but I would sooner tell you first

why it could not have been Nicky and why the confession he's just made simply can't be true."

Cirio looked at her with simmering impatience. He was thinking, it was clear, that this was merely a manœuvre to distract his attention from Nicky. But since he said nothing, Ruth went on.

" It was important to Lester Ballard, wasn't it, that everything should look as usual ? That's what you said yourself. The only unusual thing was to have been his coming home early. That couldn't be avoided. But in every other way he would have been careful to leave behind the appearance of his having done nothing exceptional. Isn't that so ? "

" Yes, yes," Cirio said, " of course."

" He wanted things to seem as if he'd simply come home from the station, left the car at the villa and then gone his usual walk up the mountain road and been killed in an accident ? "

" Yes, that's what I said."

" Then why, when he came back after throwing the other man's body into the ravine, did he put the car away in the garage ? Why didn't he leave it standing at the gate ? Cesare ! " She swung round on him.

The tip of Cesare's tongue slid along his lips. There were wary little snakes of anger and fear in his eyes. " Yes, *signorina* ? "

" Did Signor Ballard ever put the car away in the garage himself ? "

" No, *signorina*."

" You see ? " she said to Cirio. " Lester Ballard liked being waited on. He never did a thing for himself that he could tell someone else to do for him. It would have felt quite unnatural to him to drive the car back into the garage. It couldn't have occurred to him to do something so unlike himself, just at that time when it was most important to him to make everything seem as usual. He would have come back from the road to the mountains, left the car at the gate and gone straight into the house. The old woman at the shop can't see that gate, she can only see the garage. She would not have known that the car had come back. But a little later she would have seen a stranger in a brown suit and a flashy tie and perhaps a hat of some sort and sunglasses, walk down the road and steal Signorina Ranzi's car. The person who actually drove the big car back into the garage must have been somebody else and that person couldn't have been Nicky, because Nicky can't drive a car."

"You mean," Cirio said slowly, "it was the murderer of Lester Ballard, copying Ballard by putting on your clothes?"

"Of course. Lester Ballard would have come back from the mountains, left the car at the gate, come into the house, taken off my things and put on the brown suit. This other person must have been waiting and watching to see just what he was going to do. But he didn't mean to let Lester get away. At that point he attacked him with the spanner and killed him. Then this person put on my clothes and drove the car back to the garage. He had to do it, because he was meaning to put Lester's body in the car and get rid of it, perhaps also into the ravine. Then somebody walked in and upset the plan."

"Who did?"

"I did."

From Nicky there came a sound like a sob. "Don't—don't say anything, Ruth."

She went on, "I suppose I arrived just when the car had been put into the garage. Lester must have been dead already in the drawing-room. I went straight up to my room and didn't see anything. But the person must have been afraid to come back in case I heard him. Then later Nicky walked in and found his father dead. I suppose he heard me moving about in my room and so knew that I was in the house, and jumped to the conclusion that I'd killed his father. If he'd heard the whole of what I'd said to Marguerite Ranzi on the telephone in the morning, he'd have heard me saying something like that, in the way that one does say things like that when one doesn't mean them. So he made up his mind at once to try to protect me and rushed off, taking the spanner with him, all to draw suspicion on himself. Then he must have realised from the papers or from talk that he heard that this wasn't working and so he came back to confess."

"And the body?" Cirio said. "What happened to the body of Lester Ballard?"

M

The question caught her unawares. She had been talking so fast and so excitedly, and feeling so light-hearted because she herself now understood what had happened and because Nicky was not a murderer but a loving, generous, courageous boy, as she had always imagined, that she had blotted out all consideration of where her explanation was bound to lead her.

She saw Cesare smiling, a very faint, dangerous smile, while Nicky was looking at her in agony, certain that she had brought about her own destruction.

Cirio said to her quite gently, " You have said some very interesting things. But where was the body of Lester Ballard when the *maresciallo* arrived with the news of Ballard's having been found in the ravine ? "

She swayed slightly. Her brain began to spin. She saw no way out now but to tell him the truth of how she and Stephen had got rid of the body.

If only she herself had been involved, she might have gone on talking immediately. But at the idea of incriminating Stephen, she hesitated and during that short silence a sound came from some way down the road. It was the *clop*, *clop* of hoofs and the strange, groaning cry, " Aah, aah . . ." of a *carozza* driver.

A moment later a *carozza* came in sight round the bend of the road. It was driven by Giulio and its passenger was Stephen.

Ruth sprang to the railing and called out to him.

He called something back, but what he said was drowned by the violent hooting of the horn on a jeep that shot round the bend in the road, swerved around the *carozza* and stopped abruptly at the gate. Police poured out of it. One of them raced up the steps, looked round, then approached Cirio and whispered in his ear.

Cirio got up and withdrew with the man from the rest of the group on the terrace. They talked together for a minute, then Cirio returned to the table.

" Signor Ranzi, I am afraid I have very bad news for you," he said. " Your wife has been found."

Ranzi's face became rigid. He seemed not to be breathing.

" She is dead," Cirio said. " She was driving towards Salerno and her car went over the edge of the road and fell some hundred metres into the sea. She must have been killed at once."

Ranzi sat there like a stone. But then he crossed himself, while his lips moved without sound.

Stephen had come up on to the terrace and gone to Ruth's side. Ruth was shocked at herself because in such a moment as that she was capable of noticing that he had had his hair cut.

XXII

THE SIGHT of it gave her an absurd thrill of happiness. He must really love her, she thought, to have remembered such a thing at such a time. Besides, the improvement in his appearance was considerable. Somehow he looked more definite, more vigorous, less aimlessly prepared to go to seed. Yet this change had not come just from the haircut. Perhaps the haircut alone had really done no more than reveal the fact that he had a well-shaped head, a discovery which Ruth found satisfying.

But she was unable to go on thinking about these things, because Cirio turned back to her.

" I think you did not answer my question," he said. " What happened to the body of Lester Ballard ? "

She felt Stephen start. Grabbing his hand, she pressed it hard to warn him not to speak. Then to her own surprise she heard herself replying quite calmly to the question.

" I don't know what happened to it in the end," she said. " But I know what must have happened before the *maresciallo* turned up. You see, when I came downstairs because I'd heard Signor Evers knock at the door, that big green and white couch wasn't in its usual place. It had been moved to the far corner of the room. Of course, I was a bit puzzled when I saw it and I suppose if I'd stopped and thought I'd have realised that someone must have been in the room that I didn't know about. But I hadn't got murder on my mind yet. I didn't think of looking behind it to see if a body was concealed there. Which it must have been. I only thought of that after you came and looked at the back of the couch yourself. I looked at it then, after you'd gone, and I found the bloodstain."

" But when was the body moved from the house ? "

" Later the same evening. When I came back from the *Commissariat*, the couch was back in its usual place."

" And the murderer was . . . ? "

She looked across the terrace. " Cesare, it was you, wasn't it ? "

Cesare's slight body stiffened. For a moment his eyes blazed with fear, then he gave an elaborate shrug and smiled at her.

" Alas, if I could admit it for your sake, *signorina*, I would do so. I should be most happy to sacrifice myself in any way, but it happens to be impossible. I should never be able to convince the Signor Brigadiere that I was here. He knows that I spent the whole day in Naples. He will have made the most thorough inquiries and will himself be able to tell you just where I was at almost any time of the afternoon."

" That is quite true," Cirio said. " He's been vouched for by a number of people. There's no getting round it."

" In that case, Cesare," Ruth said, " tell the Signor Brigadiere how you got hold of the red note-book."

It was a daring stroke. Cesare might have the courage to say where he had found the red note-book, which, she supposed, must have been in Stephen's room during the night when Stephen had been absent. If Cesare should do this, the results for her and Stephen might be very serious.

But Cesare was frightened and he blundered. " What red note-book ? " he asked in a blustering tone. " I have no red note-book."

Ranzi came to himself. " But he has, he most certainly has," he exclaimed. " I saw it this morning in his hand. It was an address book that belonged to Lester Ballard. He always carried it about with him and consulted it whenever he wanted the telephone number of a friend or anything of that kind. If you didn't find the note-book on the body of the man he left to impersonate his corpse, then it was because Ballard wanted to take the book with him. And in that case, Cesare must have got it from the body of the real Ballard."

" No ! " Cesare shouted. " No, I didn't ! I never saw his body ! "

" Which happens," Stephen said, " to be true."

Ruth looked at him in astonishment.

" Oh, yes," Stephen said, " it's quite true. Cesare killed Signor Sebastiano, but he didn't kill Lester Ballard or even see his dead body. Cesare spent the day in Naples as he said he did. He came back after it was all over, having taken very good care to make his alibi so good that it couldn't possibly be broken. But somebody else didn't spend the day in Naples." He withdrew his hand from Ruth's and went to the railing. " Hey, Giulio ! " he shouted.

Giulio had settled himself in his carriage with his filthy green hat covering his face and apparently was already asleep. But a second call roused him. Climbing down from the carriage, he came up the steps and stood bowing to everybody on the terrace, his hat pressed against his breast. His thin, wrinkled, innocently villainous face showed an anxious yet dignified desire to please.

" You want me, *signor ?* " he said.

" Giulio," Stephen said, " would you take a careful look at that lady there and tell me if she isn't the American lady whom you drove here two days ago from San Antioco ? " As he spoke he pointed towards the door of the house.

Ruth looked incredulously where he was pointing and saw Madge Gargiulo standing in the shadow of the doorway.

Madge was wearing an overall and had her hands in its pockets. There was a grim smile on her heavy, handsome face. It seemed a little paler than usual, but that could have been the effect of her standing in the shade, when the light outside was so brilliant.

" First Cesare, now me—you're doing quite well, aren't you, love ? " she said sardonically. Her voice was as unmistakably Yorkshire as ever. " If anyone could mix me up with an American, he'd want his brain seeing to."

" Giulio, what do you say ? " Stephen asked.

Giulio went closer to her and gazed at her interestedly. He looked her up and down. He looked into her face, he studied the shape of her shoulders and her bosom, showing a simple admiration for what he saw, but no sign of recognition. Then he looked at her ankles. His expression changed. He burst into delighted laughter.

"Ha, ha, the American lady from Pompeii who couldn't get into the whore-house!" His thin, old body shook with chuckles. "Her face I don't know—she wore dark glasses. Her hair, I did not see it—she had a bright handkerchief over it. She had much red on her lips and big ear-rings. But her ankles I know. See, all those marks there. The mosquitoes they like her too well, they eat her alive. I see those scars when I help her up into my carriage and I think how sad, such scars on the ankles of such a fine woman."

"You're a liar, a damned old liar!" Madge cried furiously. "How much did he pay you to say this?"

"*Pay* me?" Giulio exclaimed as if he could not believe his ears. "He pay me five hundred *lire* to bring him up the hill and wait for him, only five hundred *lire* and that is the tariff. Pay me!"

"It's not true!" Madge cried. "I was in Naples all day with Cesare's mother."

"Yes, yes," Cesare said, "all day with my mother. My mother will swear to it."

"I'm sure she will," Stephen said. "But Signor Brigadiere"—he turned to Cirio—"I think, if you'll make further inquiries along this line, you'll find that there's no one in San Antioco who remembers seeing Signora Gargiulo getting off the train from Naples with her husband in the evening. And I think you'll find that there may be some people who travelled on the morning bus from Naples to Ravento, who remember an American lady with dark glasses and big ear-rings. She hadn't come from Pompeii as she told Giulio, telling him too that she'd wanted to see the brothel and had been refused admission, as a way of impressing that fact on his mind. She'd come from Naples, after she and Cesare had decided, during the train journey from San Antioco, what to do about Lester Ballard's intended disappearance that day. They must have found out what he was going to do, and when they saw the man in the checked shirt walking up the hill from San Antioco, they must have realised that that was the day on which it was going to happen."

"And why should I have given a curse," Madge asked

contemptuously, "whether that little rat ran off with his mistress or not?"

"But he was a valuable employee, wasn't he, Madge?" Stephen said. "You needed him and his shop and his reputation to carry out your schemes. So I don't think you'd have been happy about letting him go, even if he hadn't cheated you, as of course you'd found out, by smuggling a quantity of jewels out of the country. And so I think that when you got to Naples that morning, you sent Cesare off to his mother to arrange with her about your alibi. She was very fond of you, wasn't she? You looked after her well—she'd have done anything for you. Meanwhile, you yourself bought some sun-glasses and a scarf, which is the disguise that any woman can wear hereabouts at this time of the year, added some showy ear-rings and a phoney accent, and caught the bus to Ravento——"

"A lie, it is all a lie!" screamed Cesare in a high, shaking voice. "I did not know what she was going to do. I knew nothing of all this, nothing. She only told me she had business and she gave me a note to take to my mother. I did not know what was in the note, I thought it was only her apologies for not going to see her. I never knew, I never guessed——"

There was a report. It was like the noise of the rockets that had been bursting all the day before over San Antioco.

Cesare's face suddenly became stupid and vacant. Then with both hands clutching at his chest, his body twisted and went down in a little heap on the ground.

One of Madge's hands, which she had brought out of a pocket of her overall, had in it a small automatic pistol.

"I'm glad I did that," she said dully. "The dirty, sneaking, useless little rat—he never was any good to me. And I'm going to like doing this, too——" Raising the automatic again, she looked towards Stephen.

Another shot went off on the terrace, but it came from the revolver in Cirio's hand.

As Ruth, flinging an arm up over her eyes, felt Stephen's arms catch hold of her, Madge Gargiulo collapsed on the ground, close to the body of her husband.

XXIII

IN THE late afternoon the shadow of the cliffs slid across
the little cove. As the sparkle vanished, the bathers put
on their clothes and, in twos and threes, climbed the cliff-
path and disappeared. But the sky was still as deeply blue
as before. The water was still as warm. Its calm seemed
even to increase now that there were no bright rays of
sunshine to splinter on the ripples. The rocks still kept the
heat of the sun.

Stretched out on a flat rock, side by side, Ruth and Stephen
did not move when the other bathers left and presently
they had the place to themselves. The touch of coolness in
the air and the complete quiet were very restful. For some
time neither troubled to speak. Ruth had been half-asleep,
she did not know for how long, when at last she heard
Stephen say, " Well, d'you want the rest of it ? "

" Is there any more ? " she asked drowsily. She was
vaguely aware of questions left unanswered but none of
them seemed as important as the wonderful sense of nothing
happening.

" There are some bits and pieces," Stephen said. " They
can wait, if you'd rather."

" No, go on." She raised herself on an elbow. " But I'm
so sleepy, I may not be able to concentrate. The queer
thing is, though, I feel as if it's the first time I've been
properly awake for two days. Sleep walking, that's what I
feel as if I'd been doing. Ever since I came out on the
landing and saw Nicky."

" And it was that that you were going to tell me about
when I dashed off to look for him last night, wasn't it ? "
Stephen said.

" Of course."

" And I thought . . ."

" I know what you thought," she said. " But do you
still ? "

" N-no. No. All the same, when one considers a woman

attractive and she's living in the same house as a man like Ballard . . ."

"You're forgetting Madge."

"Ah, yes. Madge." He sat up. "I wonder which was her real reason for killing him. Was it the jewels or was it Marguerite?"

"Both, I suppose. I suppose she was his mistress," Ruth said. "Anyway, she always hated Marguerite and showed it so openly that I sometimes wondered at Lester's putting up with it. But Lester was always afraid of Madge. I can see that now, though I used to think it was just that he thought it worth his while to conciliate someone who made his life so comfortable. But what made you think of her, Stephen?"

"Giulio," he said. "He was coming down the hill, wasn't he, with his *carozza* empty, when you came out of the Ranzis' house? But then he told us that he'd been to Ravento and back that day, which meant that he'd dropped the passenger whom he'd brought with him somewhere higher up the hill. Yet there's nothing up there to interest a sight-seeing American tourist, is there? Someone of that sort would have wanted him to bring her all the way into San Antioco. So then I began to think about that tourist."

"But we'd already started on the trip to Ravento before Giulio mentioned the American woman," Ruth objected.

"Yes, but he'd already told us about having been to Ravento and I'd suddenly realised that that was an alternative route back from Naples. So I thought it was worth getting Giulio to take us to Ravento, to see if he'd talk about his passenger, whoever it had been, and also to check up the bus time-table and see if things would actually work out as I thought. Which we saw they would, as there was a bus out from Naples at just about the right time."

"So those were our real reasons for going?"

"Yes."

"Then why did you want to see Signor Sebastiano?"

"To find out if he knew anything about Madge."

"I don't suppose he did."

"Probably not," Stephen replied. "She'd always hidden behind Ballard and her husband."

"I suppose it was Madge who went to your room to look for Lester's clothes," Ruth said, "while she was supposed to be lying down in her room, feeling ill. She must have overheard me talking to you on the telephone, arranging to meet you in the *piazza*. Come to think of it, she did say once that she heard a lot of things that went on in the house. But how did Cesare get hold of the red note-book, Stephen? It nearly scared me out of my wits when I saw it."

"Did you think he'd murdered me to get it?"

"Something of the sort."

"I'd have warned you if I could," he said, "but I couldn't risk being overheard again. You see, after I'd failed to catch up with the bird-boy last night, I went back to my room and simply put all the papers invitingly on the table and then hid in that huge wardrobe to see who'd come for them. And the miserable man didn't turn up till nearly morning. I can tell you, I'll never have a really friendly feeling for a wardrobe again." Leaning forward, he rubbed both knees, as if they still ached with cramp.

Ruth rolled over, looking down into the water. It was alive with a cloud of tiny, flickering fish.

"How long will it be before they find Lester's body?" she asked.

"I shouldn't be surprised if they've found it already," Stephen said.

"But how?"

"I gave a rather pointed hint to Cirio," he said, "during that talk I had with him this morning after you and Nicky had gone into the house."

"But does that mean he knows . . . ?"

"The things that you and I did that afternoon? No, I don't think so. He may suspect some of them, but he doesn't much want to know any more than he does already."

"What about the identity of the man in the checked shirt?"

"They're going to investigate ships that have come in from Argentina. They'd thought of that all by themselves. You see, they found the tickets and the fake passports on Cesare, along with the red note-book."

"Stephen . . ." She thrust a hand into the water. In a flash, the swarm of little fish was gone and the still, green water was clear again. "You aren't going to be an easy person to trust, are you? You really do think too quickly for anyone's good."

" Perhaps marriage will put a brake on my poor brain."

" I doubt it, somehow."

" Well, perhaps getting back to a laboratory . . . Because that's where I'm going, you know. Had I mentioned it ? "

" And the book ? "

" Definitely on the scrap-heap."

Folding her arms on the rock, Ruth leant her head on them. Half-closing her eyes, she murmured, " It's going to feel queer, going back to England. No more of this sun, no more of this sky. Everything paler and greyer. I'm rather looking forward to it really, but I wonder how Nicky will like it. What are we going to do about Nicky, Stephen ? "

" We'll see how things turn out. He may not be such a problem after all. Quite a person, your Nicky."

" Yes. Things sometimes turn out queerly, don't they ? D'you know, Madge was the only person who cried when Lester was killed ? That was queer, wasn't it ? I wonder why she cried really—anger because the note-book with its precious number was lost, or had she cared for him in her way ? "

Ruth's eyes had closed. But almost immediately she opened them again.

She sat up with a jerk.

" Stephen ! The number ! "

She saw him start.

" What number ? And for heaven's sake, don't shout at me again like that, just when I'm falling asleep."

" The number in the note-book, the one that's the clue to where the jewels are hidden."

" What about it ? "

" But it's the wrong one ! You rubbed out the real one and wrote in another. Now how are the police going to trace the jewels ? "

He looked at her oddly.

" How, indeed ? " he said.

" But . . ." She stared at him aghast.

Then she saw the gleam in his eyes and began to laugh. Stephen was laughing, too.

" And they would have made such a wonderful nest-egg for us, wouldn't they ? " he said. " Rubies, emeralds, pearls . . . And just think, nobody but me knew that number—

nobody at all. But I managed to get hold of the note-book for a minute while Cirio and the others were talking and I wrote in the real number. So you can give up your dreams of living in lawless luxury in Argentina, my darling. You and I are going to pursue a very peaceful life in some London suburb."

"That sounds lovely," Ruth said. "Perfectly lovely. Only . . ."

"What's the matter now?"

"Well, I was just thinking, suppose you didn't actually remember that number correctly and the real one comes back to you sometime. . . ."

ELIZABETH FERRARS

LAST WILL AND TESTAMENT

Virginia Freer had enough on her mind already without her errant husband arriving out of the blue.

An old friend had died. There was something odd about the will. The bequests were surprising. A later, missing will was suspected. Then it turned out that the money involved was non-existent, while the most valuable remaining items had vanished from the house during the funeral.

So the presence of Felix, her charming, plausible, light-fingered con-man of a husband, back after five years absence, sprawled about the house and borrowing money, was one complication too many.

Especially when three violent deaths followed in rapid succession and the untrustworthy Felix seemed to know more about what was gong on than he had any right to . . .

'A consummate professional in clever plotting, characterisation, and atmosphere'

Washington Post

'Her great virtue, exceeding even her meatily logical plotting and gift of hitting often on really intriguing situations, is her portrayal of people'

H. R. F. Keating

HODDER AND STOUGHTON PAPERBACKS

ELIZABETH FERRARS

BLOOD FLIES UPWARDS

At least the cleaning woman was a cleaning woman.

Alison Goodrich could take some comfort from that. Because nothing else was quite what it seemed.

Consider the Eckersalls, her employers. Where did the money come from? He told a different story every day while she openly derided him and hinted, between drinks, at nameless past traumas.

The gardener. Obviously new to the job and overly concerned to describe his recent mental illness.

The secretary. Doubling all too clearly as her employer's mistress, but was that really all?

And Alison. Not the cook-housekeeper she had claimed to be at interview. Not recently deserted by her husband. Rather a woman determined to find out just what had happened to the sister who had vanished so completely and so suddenly . . .

'There are few detective story writers as consistently good as Miss Ferrars'
The Sunday Times

'Her great virtue, exceeding even her meatily logical plotting . . . is her portrayal of people'
H. R. F. Keating

'The writer who may be the closest of all to Christie in style, plotting and general milieu'
Ellery Queen Mystery Magazine

HODDER AND STOUGHTON PAPERBACKS

ELIZABETH FERRARS

A LEGAL FICTION

The Decayed Gentlewoman, they had called her as children. An unregarded painting badly in need of cleaning. Later it vanished. But before that Ginny and her mother had stopped coming to stay in Ardachoil. Colin never knew why.

Now suddenly both the Decayed Gentlewoman and Ginny had re-entered his life. An urgent station announcement at King's Cross, an oddly frantic phone call and Dr Colin Lockie, childhood emotions vividly re-awakened, found himself drawn into a maze of suspicions, theft, legal complexities and finally murder.

'Her great virtue, exceeding even her meatily logical plotting and gift of hitting often on really intriguing situations, is her portrayal of people'

H. R. F. Keating

'A consummate professional in clever plotting, characterisation and atmosphere'

Washington Post

'There are few detective story writers as consistently good as Miss Ferrars'

The Sunday Times

HODDER AND STOUGHTON PAPERBACKS